I0556332

ISLAND RENDEZVOUS
Tropical Escape, Book One

BARBARA McMAHON

Island Rendezvous
Copyright © 2011 Barbara McMahon
All Rights Reserved

No part of this book may be used or reproduced in any manner whatsoever without written permission from the author except in the case of brief quotations embodied in critical articles or reviews.

This is a work of fiction. Names, characters, places and incidents are products of the author's imagination and are used fictitiously. Any resemblance to actual events, locales, organizations or persons living or dead is entirely coincidental.

1

It was after ten when Katie knocked on the door to room 1121. It had been vacant yesterday, but according to her room list a guest had checked in last night, so she needed to get it cleaned and move on to the next one.

'Maid service,' she called as she tapped. Most of the guests were already out and enjoying the beach or the shopping. She wished she was, too. Not hearing any answer, she pulled out her passkey.

'Come in,' came from behind the door.

This guest obviously hadn't yet started out.

Using her passkey, she swung open the door and stopped in total surprise.

Her shock wasn't anything compared with that of Michael Donovan.

He'd been working on the round glass table on the balcony. When he saw Katie standing in the doorway, in the hotel's staff uniform, he rose and moved towards her, a stunned look on his face as he took in the neat, trim light blue dress with the hotel logo on the pocket, the cleaning supplies in her hands, the big cart behind her. The seconds ticked by slowly before he spoke.

'What the hell are you doing here, Katherine? You're not staying here? Is this your job?' His voice rose as he ran his gaze from her head to her sensible shoes.

She nodded, struck speechless, her heart tripping faster as

he started towards her. He was the last person she expected to see. Whatever was Michael doing here? She never expected him to leave Boston.

He towered over her as he drew closer, his six feet two inches seeming even taller than she'd remembered. He wore dark shorts and a bright blue shirt--a huge concession to the heat of Key West from a man who usually wore expensive Armani suits and silk shirts. The muscles of his chest and shoulders filled the soft cotton fabric, his stomach flat and trim. His long legs were muscular showing tanned beneath the shorts.

Sexual awareness washed through her. She'd forgotten how hot his body was. During the last months, she'd only seen him in business suits. Fully dressed, ready to face the challenges of the day.

It hadn't always been like that. She blinked away the memories of those earlier nights so long ago, though her body traitorously remembered. It had been so exciting being married to Michael—at first.

'For God's sake, Katherine, this is what you left me for? Couldn't you at least have got a better job? Something more suitable?' Anger showed on his face.

She had not seen him in over four months and this was how he greeted her. There was no 'I missed you', no 'how have you been?' just fault found with the job she'd taken. She knew it would never fit his ideal of what his wife should do. Which only went to prove she'd been right to leave. Their values and outlooks on life were too far apart to bridge.

He towered over her, anger and frustration radiating. His dark eyes glittered down at her, and a muscle jerked in his cheek.

She almost apologized, was about to offer an explanation, then a spurt of anger touched her. It really wasn't his business any longer. She had left him to make a life of her own. She wasn't answerable to him any more. He could criticize as much as he wanted; she was earning her own way and didn't need him anymore.

'There's nothing wrong with this job. It suits me for now; it's giving me time to decide what I want to do down the road. There are few demands, it's a job I can handle, the locale is like a dream—it's perfect for a transition period. What are you doing here, Michael?' she asked. She stood up as tall as she could, though he still towered over her five feet six inches, tilted her chin, the light of battle surely evident in her own brown eyes.

He had to be here for business. For the last five years that was all Michael lived for. But what business could he have in Key West? Was a new shopping complex planned? A luxury condo development? She couldn't imagine him branching out from Boston. That was where he'd gotten his first break. Where he had moved up in the construction field until his company was one of the leading firms in the area.

'You could have got a job as a social director. An art gallery director. An events planner,' he continued.

'I hate that kind of thing,' she snapped.

He was quiet a moment, his eyes searching hers.

'Was your life so hellish with me?' he asked softly, his eyes holding hers. His puzzlement clearly defined.

She hesitated a moment, then slowly shook her head. It had not always been awful—she didn't want him to think that. The first year had been wonderful, glorious. She'd been on top of the world, thinking it would never end. She'd been so happy.

And it now seemed so long ago.

'Not hellish, just... not of my choosing. I tried my best, but all those dinners, all those parties, opening nights and opera nights...everything geared to business, networking to expand Donovan Construction, make bigger deals. Making small talk with strangers who were always potential clients. Never kicking back and doing nothing.' She sighed softly. 'It wasn't my idea of a good time. I didn't have a single friend of my own. It was like forever playing a role in a play. I could go through the motions, but they were always such long, tedious evenings." She shrugged. "I'm not doing it any more.'

She broke eye contact, and glanced around the luxuriously furnished room, out through the huge sliding glass door to the beauty of the tropical island beyond the wide balcony. Palm trees swayed in the morning breeze. The colorful flowers around the grounds gave splashes of red and yellow and blue against the luscious green grass.

'What are you doing here?' she asked again.

His eyes narrowed slightly as he studied her, following the direction of her look, over the balcony railing beyond the grounds of the resort to the sparkling turquoise waters of the Gulf of Mexico.

'I came to find you.'

'The attorneys?' she guessed, with lack of surprise. She'd walked abruptly out of Michael's life several months ago, unable to continue the role of his wife. She'd tried to get him to sit down and listen to her, really hear her, but it hadn't worked.

She'd contacted him recently to make sure things were progressing with the divorce she had requested. When he'd tried to pin her down, she'd refused to talk to him, agreeing only to talk to the lawyers. Obviously they had passed on her location.

She hadn't told them she was working at the hotel, only to use it as a mailing address. No wonder Michael was shocked. It was not at all the kind of job successful Michael Donovan could be proud his wife held.

'We have nothing to talk about. I explained it to you in Boston,' she told him now.

'You explained nothing in Boston. Only some garbled tale of leaving. I told you we could discuss it,' he bit out.

'But not then—later, when it suited your very busy business schedule. You always put business first. Even before saving your own marriage.'

Did he still not understand that had been her whole complaint? He always put business first, to the exclusion of everything else. Once success had begun, it was as if he was addicted—more and more, bigger and bigger. He was never satisfied.

'I didn't notice you complaining about all the things you bought from the money that business brought in.' His anger was building.

'How would you know? You weren't ever around to hear how I liked anything.'

Katie had grown up in the last few months. She was no longer in love with the man she'd married seven years ago, nor in awe of him. She was sorry their marriage hadn't lasted, but resolved to find happiness in her new life. She'd come to terms with her situation and would no longer worry about what Michael Donovan did or said.

She glanced pointedly at the clock on the bedside table.

'I have work to do and I'm getting behind schedule; do you want your room cleaned now, or later?'

The muscle tightened in his cheek. Turning back to the balcony, he snapped out, 'Do it now.' as he stalked out and leaned both hands against the railing, his back to the room.

She quickly made the bed, washed down the bathroom and vacuumed the carpet. An odd thought popped into mind. She was doing this for her husband, something she'd hadn't done in years. It was ironic that she was doing it now that they had separated, now that she had asked for a divorce.

With his first big break, they'd bought a larger home near

Cambridge and hired a housekeeper. Frances took care of the house, the meals, taking his clothes to the cleaners. Katie had not needed to do any of the routine tasks most wives did. And that had been part of the problem. After all the years they'd been married, she felt like a visitor in her husband's house. It was only now that they were divorcing that she could do something for him herself. How odd.

She darted a glance to the balcony. Michael had turned around, leaning his back against the rails, arms crossed over his chest, staring at her. His dark eyes never left her. Watching her intensely, as if she were the only thing in the world. Flushing, she dropped her gaze to the carpet. For the second time that morning, her body warmed. Physically, they had always been compatible. More than compatible, her thoughts mocked her. He had only to touch her and she became wrapped in desire and longing. The long, passionate nights they'd shared were the things she missed the most. Even those had been infrequent during the last year.

She felt a familiar pull, an attraction of her body for his. For a moment, she felt a yearning for the way things had been. The way things had begun so long ago. At the beginning.

She moved, refusing to look at Michael again—afraid of her own reactions to him. She wished he'd stayed in Boston.

The minutes dragged by. Katie could feel his gaze follow her as she moved through her tasks. Why wouldn't he resume his work at the table, ignore her as she was so desperately trying to ignore him?

Finishing in record time, she scanned the room to make sure everything was satisfactory. While not planning to be a hotel maid forever, she took pride in her work and wanted the room to reflect it. Satisfied, she pushed the vacuum cleaner to her hall cart and let the relief take hold. She was glad to be finished—

her nerves were stretched. She hoped he was gone when she reached his room tomorrow. Why couldn't he lie on the beach like other guests?

Michael followed her to the hall.

'Finished already?'

He stood so close that Katherine could see the faint lines around his eyes. He looked so tired. Had he lost weight? She turned away, damping down her curiosity. It was no longer any business of hers.

She nodded and prepared to push the cart to the next room. His hand stopped her, resting briefly on her shoulder. Her skin tingled beneath his touch and she stepped away, her eyes wide, her heart leaping at his touch, her whole body turning to his like a magnet to true north. She watched him warily.

'Katherine...'

'I'm called Katie here, Michael. Katherine belongs to another life,' she said gently, looking away, longing to end this. She didn't want to rehash everything. She'd made the break four months ago. There was nothing to be gained by prolonging it. It had been hard to do then, and she didn't want to go through it again. Why couldn't he just let her go?

'Katie, then. When do you get off? Could we get together to talk?'

'No, I'm busy.' She pushed the cart.

'How about dinner, then?' he asked, stepping into the hall.

She threw him a look over her shoulder.

'How long are you staying here?' she asked, suddenly suspicious.

'Only a day or so. Now that I'm here, I might as well take a break from work.'

She paused a moment, but knew if he was focused in some course of action, he persevered until he got what he wanted. It was only dinner, and she could prove to herself once and for all that she could hold her own against him.

'Dinner's okay, but not here. While the hotel wants the employees to do all they can to cater to guests, that doesn't include the hired help mingling with them.' She grinned suddenly, an absurd idea striking her. 'How about pizza?'

He looked surprised and she wondered when the last time he'd had pizza. She didn't remember ever having it when they were married. How would he handle the informality of the local pizza parlor?

'Fine,' he replied.

'I'll meet you in the lobby at seven,' she told him. She went to the next room, while Michael remained in the hall staring after her until she'd entered.

Working as she did gave Katherine a lot of time to think. The routine, repetitive chores kept her hands busy, but freed her mind to consider everything. And today her mind considered Michael Donovan.

He was the last person she expected to see here on Key West. Though she knew he hadn't wanted her to leave— he'd made that clear when she'd told him of her intent–she hadn't expected him to follow her. She'd left a letter to try to explain her reasons, having been unable to get him to listen to her with his busy schedule. His so certain belief he knew what was best for everyone didn't allow him to even consider what she might have to say.

She'd wanted him to sit down with her, shut everything else away and really listen to her. But he couldn't fit her into his schedule. Finally he'd said he'd try to grab some time before the meeting with the Forrester Board on a weekend. It was the final straw.

She hadn't waited for that weekend. By then, she knew there

was nothing to talk about. Her decision had not been easily reached, but it was firm. Now she hoped she could make him see her side of things, give up and move on.

She was surprised he'd taken the time to come to Key West himself. He had always been so wrapped up in meetings and social activities tied into business, to the exclusion of everything else, that she hadn't expected him to come after her. Why had he?

Of course four months after the fact didn't exactly prove undying devotion. His schedule must have opened up at last. Now he could spare a day or two to seek out his wife. What did he hope to accomplish tonight?

Returning to Boston wasn't an option.

Michael always preferred nice restaurants with a quiet and expensive ambience. Taking him to a pizza place would give him first hand knowledge of how she'd changed. She loved the local pizza joint, the music that played, the video games teenagers played with such enthusiasm, and the laughter of families enjoying their time together. It didn't take lots of money to enjoy life—Katie had learned that since she'd been in Key West.

What if some of her new friends were at Marco's? How would she explain Michael to them? She'd never told them she'd been married. She began to have second thoughts about the whole idea. She should have told him no; why hadn't she? He'd try to talk her into coming back and she'd refuse. Why hadn't she just said no to start with?

Because she wanted to see if she could do it—have dinner and walk away knowing she'd done her best to explain her feelings. Find out why he looked so tired—had he been ill? See if there was anything to say before he left Key West. After seven years of marriage, there should be something to say.

They wouldn't need to meet each other again after that. She

didn't plan on returning to Boston. Donovan Construction had no ties to Key West; therefore Michael wouldn't be coming this way again.

It was sad. For a moment nostalgia threatened to overwhelm her. They'd been so happy when they'd first married. She had been so in love with him, so proud he'd chosen her for his wife. But gradually his work had grown more demanding, his goals more lofty, until Michael rarely spent any time with her unless it was at the endless round of parties and social events designed to further the interests of Donovan Construction.

Which it had. The firm had grown by leaps and bounds. From luxury homes, to low-rise office buildings, to shopping malls, Donovan's was known to be the best in the Tri-State area.

Dinner tonight would not expand the business. What would they even talk about once she made it clear she was content doing what she was doing, making friends, furnishing her apartment the way she wanted?

Katie's small apartment was only a dozen blocks from the hotel, on a quiet side street. Her heart lifted every day as she started her walk home. The sun was warm on her back, the air gently stirring in the afternoon breeze—enough to give an illusion of coolness, though the hot sun belied it. Her eyes scanned the colorful stands and boutiques that lined Duval Street—Old Key West's main street—enjoying the bright colors of the wooden buildings with their fancy gingerbread trim; the variety of merchandise available for tourists and natives alike: bright T-shirts, shells of every color, and the profusion of flowers.

She'd deliberately sought a warm climate, looking for a place that was as different from Boston as she could find to start over. She wanted a less formal lifestyle, with people ready to be friends and easy to get along with. Kicking off the traces, she wanted a totally different life. She'd found it in Key West.

Katie enjoyed her walks to and from work, discovering new sights each day with the gardens of the homes she passed, or the displays the shops put out. She loved greeting the shopkeepers as she passed, buying some fresh fruit at one of the vendor's stands each morning. The fresh air and exercise brought a new freedom to her body. Key West was small enough so that she could walk almost everywhere, from the beach to work, to the stores.

The change from the frigid Boston winter was so novel that she was constantly surprised and delighted. Boston was freezing in February, but in Key West the balmy days were ideal—warm and sunny. Occasionally they had rain, but it was not a dreary, cold rain like that of Boston winters, but warm, almost like a shower to freshen the flowers. Some afternoons she danced on her small balcony in the rain. The water was refreshing and sweet. Everything was colorful, casual and fun. She was glad she'd chosen Key West to start over.

The foot traffic on Duval was heavy at this time of the afternoon. Bronzed men and women in scanty attire lounged at the pavement cafes. Sun burnt tourists gazed at the offerings of the shops along the way. Royal palms offered spots of shade on the hot pavements. Here and there a courtyard offered a glimpse of cool garden serenity in the sultry afternoon. The soft breezes that constantly blew from the water caressed her cheeks, tossed the short curls on her head and cooled her skin.

She turned on to her street. Bougainvilleas climbed the wall to her right, its bright purple flower a vibrant contrast to the stark whitewash of the wall. It was a wide, quiet street lined with big old houses, some of which had been converted into flats. The street had called to her when she'd first seen it—she'd known her place was in one of the converted houses.

In only minutes she opened the door to her apartment, crossing quickly to the french doors, throwing them wide to the afternoon breeze. Bright pots of flowers lined her small balcony, giving more color and fragrance each day. She loved her view— a glimpse of the blue water to the right, the green of the neighbor's lawn to the left and everywhere the tall, stately palms swaying against the azure sky. It was quite a change from Boston.

She surveyed her small apartment, pleased anew by what she saw. She'd furnished it cheaply, buying things second-hand from garage sales, using pretty, crisp blue and white gingham to cover the mismatched pieces, giving the room a coordinated look. Starched white curtains framed the windows. There were few extras for decorations—no pictures, no knick-knacks. Yet her apartment was comfortable and welcoming.

Life on Key West was vastly different from the opulent life she'd led in Boston. She didn't miss any of that hectic pace. The friends she'd made here lived in circumstances similar to her own. They liked simple pleasures and proved to Katie what she'd often suspected in the past–that money wasn't needed to make people happy.

Maybe money even caused unhappiness. Look at her own life. The aunt who had raised her had money, but no husband, no children of her own, stuck with her sister's child whom she relegated to nannies and boarding school.

Michael had no real interests beyond work, earning money to spend it on material things, not for enjoyment, but to impress. Katie had come to believe experiences meant more than material things. She relished each day with new experiences tumbling over themselves.

Pampered—yes, Katie has been pampered from birth. Her aunt had been one of the Boston Brahmins–old family, old money. She'd raised her niece in elegant splendor, constantly emphasizing Katie's place when she was home. Making sure she attended all the right schools.

Michael had taken over when they'd married, sheltering her from everyday life as surely as if she'd been in a cocoon. She'd never given much thought to earning her own living. She wasn't sure now what she would do with the rest of her life, but she'd broken free from the past and was making a new start. Something would turn up, but for now, she was content to make beds and spend her free time at the beach.

She needed to take the next step and make sure the divorce went through. She'd get that assurance from Michael tonight.

She changed quickly, and went to meet one of her friends—they were going snorkeling. Debbie had been at the hotel the longest of any of her new friends—over four years. She'd introduced Katie to snorkeling. Love at first sight! Katie went whenever she could. Grabbing her gear, she headed out.

She walked the several blocks to the beach. She found this the loveliest time of day at the beach—the late afternoon. The sand was soft and white, imported; she'd been told, from Barbados. Fringed with coconut palms and leafy mango trees, this particular beach was not large, but beautifully contrasted with the varied blues of the sea. The coconut palms, laden with fruit, stretched out towards the water, their spots of shade providing welcome relief from the blazing sand. Only the tourists exposed themselves to its full rays of the sun and heat of the sand.

The Gulf of Mexico was warm and crystal-clear. Beneath its surface the bright, colorful tropical fish darted and swam in the pristine water. The yellows and blues of angelfish and butterfly fish showed clearly against the light sandy bottom. She often dived from the beach. Whenever they could afford it, she and her friends joined a group on a boat and dived out by the reef. The pretty coral formations were a fascinating delight to Katie. Their lacy fans, pink and yellow colors and intricate designs enchanted her. She never tired of exploring.

The first time Katie'd wanted to go to the reef and ran into a money issue she'd realized how different her life would be in the future. As Michael Donovan's wife, she could afford anything. As Katie Harrington, newly single, recently arrived in Key West, she had to watch her expenses and budget carefully.

She greeted Debbie when she arrived and before long they were in the water exploring the bounty beneath the gentle waves. This was her idea of the perfect life.

Katie was later returning home than she'd planned, and she rushed through a quick shower, dressing at warp speed, drawing on a colorful pink and rose cotton sundress that hugged her body and flared at the waist. It was cool and comfortable. She dried her hair, applied a touch of mascara and was ready. Not wanting to be late meeting Michael, she hurried the few blocks to the hotel, arriving flushed and out of breath.

Michael was already in the lobby, looking remote and withdrawn in dark trousers and a light shirt opened at the throat—casual for him, but almost formal by Key West standards. When he spotted her, he smiled, the corners of his eyes crinkling, his face looking younger.

Suddenly she realized he'd rarely smiled over the last five or six years— work was too serious. For a moment, it looked as if he was glad to see her. Katie marveled at the transformation and involuntarily smiled back. He looked a different man than the dedicated hardcore businessman she knew—younger, relaxed, attractive.

More like the man she'd married seven years ago.

Her heart sped up a little as she hurried toward him and the worries over dinner disappeared.

He stepped out to meet her, his eyes running slowly down the length of her, taking in her shiny blonde sun-streaked hair, the light gloss on her lips, down her long legs to her sandal-clad feet. She felt his gaze as if he touched her. Again that curious warmth permeated her body and made her breathless. She felt the tingling awareness of her body for his.

'Prompt, I see,' was all he said, though from the light in his eye Katie thought he wanted to say more.

'I try to be,' she replied. 'Are you sure you want pizza?' Doubts surfaced again. They had never had a casual evening at a fast-food place before. It had always been dinner at Pierre's, La Belle Fleur or some other expensive restaurant in Boston. Even if they ate at home, Frances had served.

'I'm looking forward to it,' he told her.

Katie was halfway across the lobby when his warm hand grasped her upper arm, bringing her to a halt. Michael stepped before her.

'Good grief, Katherine, that outfit is positively indecent. The air-conditioning makes your nipples hard and they show right through that top. Every man in the place is staring at you.'

Katie glanced down, Oops—he was right. But surely not every man was looking at her. Not with all the other women dressed to kill in the hotel. She darted a quick glance around the lobby; no one was even looking their way.

She shrugged. 'Let them look. It's really not your business any more, is it?'

He frowned, not liking her reply.

'No need to ask how you've been—you look radiant, though not like the sophisticate I knew. You've cut your hair,' he said. Was that his way of trying to start a conversation?

He reached out as if to touch the soft blonde curls. Katie instantly shied away, not wanting the intimacy that his touch would imply. She peeped up at him; his look was yearning, hungry. Had he actually missed her? Or was she reading something into his look she wished might be there?

'How have you been, Michael?' Katie felt a tingling at her arm, against the side of her breast where the back of his fingers touched. This was Michael, the husband she was leaving. His touch should have no meaning to her. But she had trouble thinking of anything else. She stepped back to break contact and he released her arm, slowly pulling his fingers free. She felt his warmth long after he no longer touched her.

'I've been fine.' The words were clipped, the tone brusque.

She looked closely again. He looked tired and leaner. Working too hard, she surmised.

'I've missed you.' His voice was strained; his dark eyes never left hers.

'No, Michael, you haven't,' she said gently. 'You might have missed the wife who did your bidding without complaint, who helped at all your social events. But you couldn't have missed me—you don't even know me.'

He stared at her for a long moment. 'You may be right that we're not as close as we could be. I can remedy that. I'll call the office, postpone a few things. We can go on a cruise together, before I have to be back for the Murdock deal, get to know one another again...'

His voice trailed off as Katie shook her head, slowly but definitely.

'There you go again, Michael. I don't want to go on a cruise. I want to stay right here. I'm happy here. There's nothing more for us, and you can't keep running my life as if I were some employee of yours. Are you ready to go to dinner?'

As they walked down the street, twilight began to fall. The store lights illuminated the walkway and one bright star could be seen hanging just above the horizon.

Michael glanced down at Katie again. 'Have you changed your dressing habits here, or was this for me?'

He ran his fingers down her back. She felt his touch with a shock. His fingertips were light, leaving a trace of electricity in their wake. She shivered and blushed, darting him a quick glance. She was surprised at his gesture, even more so at her reaction. Seeing the gleam in his eyes as he met hers, she caught her breath. Her heart skipped a beat, then began tripping double time. The trail his fingers left was warm, her skin clamored for further contact. In fact her whole body clamored for contact with his. She had to clear her throat to speak. This was madness. Why had she agreed to this evening?

'Actually just no bra. It's so hot and humid here, I usually don't wear one...' She trailed off. There was no need to explain to him. She was living her own life now.

'Are you sure you want pizza?' she asked again. She couldn't imagine Michael dealing with trailing strings of cheese. The way-ward blob of marinara sauce, or an errant mushroom. He was always so fastidious. Maybe it hadn't been such a good idea to suggest Marco's. 'Maybe you'd like to go somewhere else? They have some nice seafood places here.'

'I assure you, Kathe—er—Katie, that I shan't embarrass you by not knowing how to eat pizza. I do have some social graces.' His tone was dry.

'Oh, Michael, I never thought you would embarrass me, I only thought it wouldn't be as enjoyable as some other food.' She was surprised that he'd read her mind. 'Pizza is so casual, and we never ate it in Boston.'

'I didn't know you liked it,' he said.

'Yes.' What more could she say? It pointed out even further how far apart they were.

Customers seated themselves at Marco's and Michael waited for Katie to lead the way. She chose a quiet booth at the back. The ones surrounding it were unoccupied, giving them momentary privacy. Katie had feared several of her friends might be at the restaurant, but she saw no one she knew. Unconsciously, she relaxed. She didn't know how she would explain Michael to them. She felt as nervous as a teenager on a first date.

While they waited for their order, Katie faced him across the table. 'How long are you staying?'

'That depends on you.'

'Why come at all? The time for talking is gone.' She put her hands in her lap, gripping them together to hide her nerves.

'I disagree. Isn't that why we're here? Let's order. What do you like?' he said. They agreed on a combo and Michael went to the counter to order a small pizza. He bought a large pitcher of beer. He did not seem at all out of place in the casual restaurant, Katie thought as she watched him. He always seemed perfectly at home in the most elegant restaurants in Boston; shouldn't he be just a little out of his element here?

'How did you get your job?' he asked when he sat down and placed the pitcher and mugs on the table.

Stalling, Katie poured them each a glass full and then set the pitcher down. 'I don't have many marketable skills. A fine art degree doesn't really prepare anyone for an easy way to make a living. Maid work was all I could find. But I don't plan to keep it forever. Just till I get on my feet and decide what I want to do.'

'And what might that be?' The muscle in his cheek jerked as he watched her. She could tell he was still angry. Could she continue?

'I'd like to do something in business. Maybe open a small

shop with island jewelry, shells, driftwood, the kind of things tourists would like.' Her enthusiasm was damped down by his glittering look. She stopped. That was all she'd say. He didn't have to lecture her on how impractical it might be. Or inquire as to where she would find the start up money, or the knowledge to run a business.

Their pizza arrived and Katie welcomed the diversion.

'I want you to come back, Katherine. It's not the same with you gone,' he told her once the waitress had deposited the pizza plates.

'I'm not coming back.' She took a wedge of pizza, pulling it free from the pie, draping the cheese trailers on top as she put it on her paper plate. He couldn't make her do anything. Not unless he used force—and Michael would never do that.

'You can't expect me to believe you don't miss what we had in Boston,' he said watching her.

She stared at him, wondering exactly what he meant. She didn't miss the house, or Frances, or the endless social events for Donovan Construction. But she did miss him. Missed the love they'd shared at first, the laughter, the lovemaking.

Katie's face grew warm. She could never admit to that. Some day she'd find someone else who could make her feel the way Michael had.

Maybe.

His gaze held hers and for one panicked moment she wondered if he'd read her mind. He always had such power to excite her, enthrall her, pleasure her.

She broke eye contact and reached for her drink. There was more to life than that, and she wanted it—love. She wanted to be first in someone's life. She wanted her opinion sought and listened to. She wanted laughter with shared amusement. Enjoyment in each other's company—not artificial social gatherings more to move business along than to enjoy friends.

'Hi, Katie, I thought it was you.' Jim Reed stopped by the table and greeted her with a grin. He was one of her new friends. He was the only one who was passionately driven to get ahead, to make more money, become a business success. He worked at the local bank, was the only native islander of her group of friends, and was dying to move north and make it big. Jim always had his eye on the main chance. In that he was similar to Michael. Well, maybe without quite the drive Michael had.

He stood at the end of the booth, looking inquisitively at Michael. Katie wondered idly if her husband could help him, and looked over at him with the thought. Dare she ask him later? Would he scoff at her requesting a favor when trying to end their marriage?

'Hi, Jim. Michael, this is Jim Reed, one of my friends here on Key West. Jim, Michael Donovan—uh—a friend of mine from Boston.'

Michael's face held a smile, his eyes a knowing glint. The intent of the introduction had not escaped him.

Jim was obviously curious about Michael. In the nicest way imaginable Michael sidestepped the questions Jim posed. Katie was impressed. He did nothing to depress Jim's spirits, yet revealed very little about himself, and Jim finally realized defeat and rejoined the group he'd come with.

Katie was surprised that Michael hadn't snubbed her young friend. She smiled at him warmly. 'Thank you.'

'Was I ever that young, dumb and obvious?''

She shrugged. In the early days, Michael had been very much like Jim.

'A little young for you, isn't he?' Michael said softly.

She bristled. Not everything was about sex. 'Jim's just a friend, Michael. Anyway, he's only a year younger than I am.'

As they ate, Katie couldn't help noticing Michael fit in. He seemed to enjoy the food, and didn't seem as out of place as she'd expected. She'd been foolish to worry about his reaction to one of her new favorite places.

And why shouldn't he fit in? she thought. He hadn't built up Donovan Construction by riding roughshod over people. He had to deal with all types—from bankers and other investors to real-estate moguls, to carpenters and bricklayers. And he did it successfully. It was a skill he had perfected. He could fit in anywhere, be comfortable, and make others feel comfortable as well.

He told her about some of the people she knew, what the business had been doing.

She listened with half an ear. She didn't care anymore. Her eyes roamed around the restaurant, smiling at a family with small children making a mess of their pizza. One little boy ate his slice upside down, with the toppings falling off.

Neither brought up the separation or divorce.

When they finished, he asked, 'Ready to go?'

She nodded and slid from the booth. The evening was almost over. She once again felt as if she were treading on eggshells. They still needed to talk about their own situation. Had he held off to make dinner pleasant?

They walked back to the hotel. The night air was refreshing after the hot day. The slight breeze blowing in from the ocean tinged the air with salt. Katie caught the scent of night-blooming jasmine, its sweet fragrance adding to the romance of the evening. She darted a quick glance at Michael. Did he feel the romance of Key West?

He walked beside her, his eyes examining the street as they ambled along, noting the bars with music spilling across the pavement, the small cafes filled with diners, the other strollers along the avenue. Key West had a festive, laid-back feel all year long. Katie had only been here a few months, but she had fallen in love with it.

'Which way?' he asked when they stopped at a pedestrian crossing.

'Straight ahead. I'm beyond the hotel. But you don't need to see me home—I'll be fine on my own, it's only a few blocks from the hotel.'

He started to say something, then paused, shrugging. 'Fine. I enjoyed meeting your new friend, Kath—Katie. Different from our friends back in Boston, but interesting none the less.'

Katie was silent, not knowing if he was being condescending or truthful in his comment. She almost corrected him about 'their' friends, but not wanting to disturb the end of what had turned out to be a pleasant evening, she kept quiet.

She smiled ruefully in the dark; still the polite socially correct Bostonian. Why didn't she just tell him she didn't consider the people she'd dealt with in Boston her friends, but just others who could benefit Donovan Construction?

But he'd be gone soon; she'd be free. She'd hold her tongue a little longer.

He stopped in the shadows at the edge of the light shining from the hotel lobby. For a moment Katie thought he meant to kiss her goodnight. Panic engulfed her. She didn't want him to kiss her; she only wanted him to leave her alone—to return to Boston and let her continue with her new life in Key West.

But Michael didn't kiss her, only drew his fingertips lightly over her satiny cheek. Her skin tingled and she felt the shock to her toes. Eyes wide, Katie tried to see his expression, but it was dark where they stood, and she couldn't see him clearly.

'Goodnight,' he said.

'Aren't we going to talk?' she asked, surprised at the abrupt end.

'Another time.'

'Goodnight then.' Disappointment and relief washed

through her. They ended the evening almost as friends. Yet if he didn't leave, they'd still have to discuss their divorce.

Michael's touch had stunned her—she'd felt it to her toes and she had no business reacting like that. She'd thought he would kiss her and was disappointed when he hadn't. What was the matter with her?

Right before she fell asleep, she tried to picture when they'd discuss the divorce. So far they hadn't resolved anything at all.

2

Despite the turmoil of her thoughts when she went to bed, Katie slept well and awoke at her normal early hour. Donning a dark blue one-piece bathing suit under shorts and a shirt, she slipped out to the beach for a quick swim before work.

The sun was just rising; the water sparkled as the rays struck it. The blues of the sea were dark and mysterious in the early morning light. The palms were still, the beach deserted except for a lone runner in the far distance. Katie dropped her towel, shrugged out of her shorts and shirt and waded in.

As always the warmth of the ocean surprised her. The only time she'd gone in swimming at Cape Cod she'd been cold—and that had been in July. Here it was February and the water was warm, only a few degrees cooler than the air. It was heavenly. She swam, floated and gave herself up to the pleasures of the sea.

There was rarely much surf on Key West—the water lapped the shore much like lake water. Here and there she saw a brightly colored fish darting through the clear shimmer of the sea. She should have brought her snorkeling equipment. But she only had time for a quick swim, not get lost in exploring beneath the surface.

Refreshed, she waded ashore, scanning the skyline from the beach. To the left was the Southernmost Marker—a spot tourists loved. Everyone wanted his or her picture taken there, the south-ernmost point in the contiguous forty-eight states. To her right through the palms and trees she glimpsed the top of the old lighthouse. The morning was quiet, peaceful and still. The soft muffled slaps of the wavelets only added their soothing sounds to the restful scene. The sky was cloudless, deep blue, the air still and scented with the salt.

Idly she watched the runner approach as she reached for her towel. She recognized him with some surprise; it was Michael. He was wearing running shoes, a brief pair of shorts and had a towel draped around his neck. His hair was damp from sweat and his strong body gleamed in the early sun.

He was surprised to see her and stopped running to walk closer, mopping his face with his towel.

'Good morning,' Katie said, draping her towel around her. 'I didn't expect to see you up and out so early.'

'I usually run early in the morning. Helps keep my body tuned for the rigors of business,' he told her.

She stared at him in surprise. 'Even in Boston?'

He nodded, his eyes narrowed as he watched the emotions play across her face. 'For the last couple of years, anyway.'

Katie's first reaction was dismay. How could she have lived in the same house with this man and never known something so basic as he ran every morning?

Then the implications hit her. It was for that reason and oth-ers that they were separating. They did not have a marriage, a sharing of two lives. That was the real sadness of it all—not some-thing she wanted to deal with this early in the day.

'Do you come swimming every morning?' Michael asked, glancing around the deserted beach. 'Isn't it dangerous to swim alone?'

'I'm careful.' She hadn't meant for her tone to be defensive, but Michael was one of several people giving her the same advice. Well-meaning, she was sure, but she was out to live her own life in her own way and didn't need others telling her what to do.

Michael's breathing had slowed and the perspiration dried on his skin. Tugging on the ends of the towel, he looked down the beach.

Katie dropped her eyes. She had the craziest desire to run her hands over his shoulders and chest, tangle her fingers in the dark mat of hair that covered the strong muscles of his chest, tapering to disappear in the waistband of his shorts; to feel his warm skin, his muscles move beneath her fingers. She was cool, drying off in the early day, and would like his warmth to envelop her.

'Well, I won't keep you—I know you want to be off running,' she broke the silence, wrapping her towel around her shoulders and wanting to say more, yet not knowing how; wanting to stare at his body, but afraid to give herself away by glancing at him.

'See ya.' With that abrupt statement, Michael started off, never looked back, though Katie watched him until he was a small dot in the distance. He ran with grace and power and she remembered how fit his body was.

She thought about what she'd learned of Michael later that morning while she cleaned her rooms. They hadn't shared a bedroom the last few years, so she wouldn't have known he arose early each day to run. Working late, Michael hadn't wanted to awaken her when he came to bed, so he'd moved to another bedroom almost three years ago, visiting her when the mood presented itself. She rarely arose in Boston before seven. By the time she appeared for breakfast, Michael had already departed for work. What other aspects of his life did she not know about?

In reviewing their marriage, she had to admit they'd spent less and less time together. At first, they'd spent every free moment together planning, dreaming, loving. But as Michael focused more on building his business, putting in long hours, doing everything he could to get ahead, to make Donovan Construction one of the most important companies in the Boston area, their special time shrank. He had succeeded, while she sat at home alone. Then, more recently, still not satisfied, he had kept busy expanding it—keeping it on track, as he said.

She hadn't minded at first; she'd been in awe of what he was accomplishing. She had been anxious to do her part. Which he insisted she did with the entertainment. But the business was never big enough, never successful enough. And she had grown so tired of meaningless chatter with people she partied with only for business.

She couldn't pinpoint when they became almost like strangers. He rarely spoke of business to her, actually rarely spoke to her at all in the last year, except to check in for planned social events.

'Neither did you try to find out. Not once did you seek him out and try to make the marriage different, make it more like what you wanted,' she mumbled as she replaced a pillowcase. She'd gone along with things the way they were. She hadn't spoken to him about how she felt, what she thought. Desultory conversation at dinner centered on what charity she'd worked on, what Mrs. Winthrop said, or who would be coming to the next social event where Michael wanted to impress someone.

Years ago she might have been able to do something, had she had the nerve then. Now it was too late. She was happy in her new life, she told herself firmly. The years in Boston seemed almost like they happened to someone else.

The next room on her floor was Michael's. She paused, took a deep breath and knocked.

He swept the door open, a smile in his eyes for her. He had obviously showered since his run, and his hair was gleaming in the morning light. He wore only shorts, no shirt. His skin was lightly tanned over the muscles of his arms and chest; the dark mat of hair was crisp and curly.

'I've come to do the room, if it's convenient now?' she said breathlessly, unable to look away. Why was she having trouble with her breathing? He seemed too close.

'Sure, come on in.' He stepped back only a little, and Katie had to squeeze in, brushing against his hard chest in passing. She bit her lip, trying to ignore the tingling sensation that touching his warm skin wrought.

She started her cleaning in the bathroom. Michael leaned lazily against the door, watching her, his arms crossed over his chest. Self-conscious with him following her every move, Katie grew clumsy, having to take extra time and care to do the job right.

'Do you have to stand there?' she asked, finally turning to him in exasperation.

'No, but I want to. Why?' His dark eyes laughed at her, as if he knew he was making her nervous, and didn't care. Provocatively he didn't move.

'Go out to the beach,' she ordered, forgetting that he usually told her what to do, forgetting he was a guest. He was exasperating and she wanted him out of her way.

'I like it right here.' His voice was low, sexy.

Katie scowled, and resumed her work. He blocked the door. She stretched out her cleaning as long as she dared, always conscious of his eyes following her every move. Would he move or make her ask? Damn it, couldn't he see he was causing her trouble?

Eventually she took a deep breath and started for the door; her eyes met his briefly then looked away. She had to do the bedroom, and quickly, or she would get behind schedule. Would he let her pass? Or was he having too much fun boxing her in the bathroom?

Michael remained where he was, a devilish look on his face. He seemed to be daring her to move him, to push past him and get on with her work.

Katie paused, almost touching him, then boldly walked on, bumping straight into him. He allowed himself to be pushed out of the way with no resistance at all. She frowned; he was teasing her. She chanced a glance at him, flustered at the lazy grin she saw, the assessing gleam in his eye.

She swallowed hard. She didn't know how to handle this. Michael had never teased her before. She darted another quick look in his direction. He was watching her intently.

She dusted the dressing table, the table and chairs, conscious all the while of his steady regard. The tangled sheets of the bed gave rise to visions of Michael sleeping on the cool sheets. She knew he slept nude and the image of him in the bed was vivid. His tanned skin would look even darker in comparison to the light percale sheets.

His arms and legs would be spread out, taking more room than his share. Self-consciously she straightened out the sheets, her mind filled with memories of the man beside her. She tried to blink the images away.

As she made the bed he moved closer to her, laughter lurking in his eyes.

'Aren't you worried about unruly guests when you go into occupied rooms?' he asked.

She pulled the bedspread smooth. 'No, usually the rooms are empty. If not, I can take care of myself.'

'Show me.'

He reached out and pulled her around to face him, his hands firm on her arms, but not tight. As he lowered his face his voice was low. 'You're more beautiful than ever and you're slipping away from me. I don't want that to happen. I want you, Katherine.'

Before she could react, his lips covered hers and Katie was lost. His mouth was hot and firm, pressing against her with passion and longing she hadn't felt in years. His hands moved to encircle her, draw her up against him, against the warm, hard muscles of his chest, into the circle of his strong, demanding arms.

She clung to his shoulders as she delighted in the fevered feelings he evoked with his lips, the erotic touch of his tongue. Her fingers reveled in the strength found beneath his warm skin, seeking to learn him again, tracing muscles and delighting as they moved beneath her. Gently his tongue teased her lips until she gave in and opened them slightly.

Joy exploded within her as his tongue explored the soft recesses of her mouth and dueled with hers, tantalizing and tormenting her until she wanted more, much more. She grew bold and returned his kiss, her own senses inflamed, her tongue moving with a will of its own, her lips moving, responding, tasting him.

She should have been pushing him away, but instead she caressed his shoulders, entwining her fingers in his thick dark hair, as she strained to get closer to assuage the fiery longing that arose. She was caught up in a maelstrom of feelings and wanted to ride the wave as far as she could go. The warmth from his chest heated her through the thin cotton of her uniform, the material a barrier she wished gone.

He drew her against him, pushing her hips forward to meet the rising need of his. Katie lost track of time and reality, her senses spinning, her body awakening to demands and desires long dormant. Hungrily she reached for more.

The shrill noise of the bedside phone ended the spell. Slowly Michael raised his head, his eyes half closed, his breathing ragged. He looked down at Katie for a long second, then slowly put her from him as the insistent clamor of the phone shattered the moment.

'Mark my place,' he said, putting a finger on her lips, then reached around her to answer the phone.

Katie watched him with dazed eyes, panting in the hot room. It was as if she had been transported back in time to the first heady days of their marriage. It took her a moment to regain her thoughts; her mind was spinning. What had happened? What had she allowed to happen? She had to get out of here or everything would be lost. She was stunned at her loss of control, at how easily she'd forgotten her resolve to leave and start anew. She acted like some teenager in the throes of first love. Damn him, she'd told him it was over. Was that his way of trying to show it was not?

Turning, she made a last swipe on the bed and rushed to the hall. She'd forget the vacuuming. If he reported her, so be it. Pushing her cart frantically down the hall, she skipped two rooms and parked the cart between another two.

Trusting he would not pursue her, she let herself into one of the rooms and closed the door behind her. It was against all rules of the hotel. Maids were to leave the door open so there was no suspicion of wrongdoing. But right now she didn't want to see anyone, or have them see her. Grateful these guests had left for the day, she moved on shaky legs to the bed, sinking down on the end, her breathing gradually coming under control.

She closed her eyes; her lips were still throbbing from his kiss, her heartbeat increasing as she remembered every detail. Lightly, she ran her tongue over them. His taste still lingered.

This was madness.

Her ears straining to hear any sounds from the hall, she stood and quickly went through the motions of her job, forcing her hands to work efficiently, blocking the thoughts that clamored for attention, going through the routines of the day. When she was finished in that room, she paused by the door and took a deep breath. Slowly she eased open the door. Peeking down the hall, she saw it was deserted. She dumped the dirty linen into the cart, took the vacuum and quickly cleaned the carpets before moving to the next room, dashing in to close the door behind her.

Her shift seemed endless. Never before had she been impatient for it to end. But today she wanted to get away, as far away from the hotel as fast as she could.

She didn't want to see Michael again. She was afraid of her reactions if she did.

How dared he kiss her the way he had? She'd felt consumed by his kiss, the excitement of his touch. It wasn't fair; she'd made her decision and he had no right to come to Key West and play on her emotions. Their marriage was over.

How could she have reacted as she had? Her cheeks warmed. How could she not respond as she had to the magic that was Michael?

At last all her rooms were finished, even the ones adjacent to Michael's. When she had ventured back, his door was firmly shut. She was quick and thorough and left the vacuuming for last lest he hear her. Once finished, she fled to the housekeeping area. The day had seemed forty hours long, but it must have been of normal duration because the other maids were changing and chattering casually, tossing their uniforms into the laundry.

Only as she walked home did she let herself dwell on the memory of his kiss. A slow bud of desire grew within her at its memory. It had been an exciting kiss, provocative. She hadn't wanted it to stop. But why was he kissing her now? Seems like he could have paid a bit more attention last fall or last summer. Why today of all days?

His statement just before the kiss—did that provide a clue? He thought her beautiful. But he had often said that, his tone as impersonal as if he had been admiring a piece of sculpture. She had done her best to look beautiful for him. It was what he wanted and expected and she had tried to fulfill her part of their marriage. The clothing and make-up she'd used had all been to that end.

But he hadn't said he never wanted her before. Not with that sexy masculine voice. Sexy, successful Michael Donovan had wanted her, even if only for a moment, in his room this morning. The passion in his voice had shown the strength of his feelings. Had the phone not rung would he have seduced her? It would not have been very hard if he had continued to kiss her like that.

Panic rose within her. She simply could not allow that. It would be better to stay away from Michael Donovan. She dare not let herself become involved with him emotionally—it would be too hard to let him go a second time if she did.

And Katie still wanted to let him go. She was leading the kind of life she wanted. There was so much to do on Key West and she was doing exactly what she wanted, when she wanted.

She had never been as physically active as she had these last months. The work at the hotel was demanding. She'd quickly discovered that her new friends loved the outdoor life offered by Key West's fine climate. Sports like swimming, snorkeling, cycling, and volleyball had soon filled Katie's free time. Walking everywhere was different, too. She couldn't afford a car, and fortunately didn't need one on the island. It was small and self-contained, and everything she needed was in walking distance. She'd grown tanned, strong, and her spirits soared.

When she reached her apartment, she changed her clothes and headed for the beach; with luck, she'd find some friends there. Someone she knew was always hanging out, to swim with, or for a pick up game of volleyball.

When she arrived, the sandy shore was crowded. Tourists who had come south to escape the harsh northern winters loved the sunny white beaches of Key West and spent many hours each day soaking up the warmth. She preferred it when they used the resort beaches. But couldn't fault them for loving this one. She did.

Quickly she scanned the crowd, seeing the volleyball net being strung in the distance. She wandered over and found several of her friends, including Marlise, Charlie and Jody, ready to start a game. The others she didn't know, but it didn't matter—the important thing was that they were all out for a good game of volleyball. And by the time the game ended, they'd be friends.

Katie wore her white bikini, preferring to sunbathe while doing something, rather than lie on the sand and do nothing. Greeting her friends, she quickly discarded her cover-up and joined in. She hit a ball over; it was returned. Marlise hit it almost straight up. Katie lunged for the assist, and Marlise tripped and fell back just as Katie dived for the ball, returned it and fell full length beside Marlise. She raised her head, laughing. Marlise and the others were laughing, too.

'Point,' Charlie yelled, then reached out a hand to help the two girls to their feet. Katie shook her head; the short curls bouncing, the sand falling from her like rain.

'You all right?' he asked.

'Yes,' she giggled again. 'Great save, right?' She was proud of her return, since she had only learned volleyball since arriving at Key West.

'Right on,' Charlie agreed.

As she brushed the sand off, her eyes caught sight of a tall figure standing on the grassy edge of the beach some yards away—Michael Donovan.

The smile wiped from her face. The old familiar nervousness welled up, her heart started beating heavily as she stared at him, her breathing suspended. What was Michael Donovan doing here? Couldn't she escape anywhere? Was he following her?

'Damn it,' she muttered, anger building to cover her uncertainty. How dared he come down here and interfere? He didn't have to intrude in every aspect of her life. If he did anything to ruin her new life she'd never forgive him.

His eyes glittered at her, as he watched her from his vantage-point, flicking down the length of her, pausing briefly at her breasts, her hips, taking in the short blonde curls, the deep tan, dark brown eyes. She flushed, extremely conscious suddenly of the amount of skin the bikini exposed. It barely covered her firm body, the swell of her breasts straining the stretchy white material, the pants low and daring.

Katie felt self-conscious under his regard, and underdressed.

What must I do to get rid of you? she screamed internally. She hadn't been on her own long enough. She still lacked the self- confidence she wanted to deal equably with this powerful man. In business he could be ruthless. Was he planning to attempt to get his way in this as well? She could feel the pull of attraction she'd always felt for him. She resisted—she must resist.

She turned back to the game, throwing herself into activity, a delightful grin painted on her face. She'd show Michael that her new life was fun and exactly what she wanted. She would ignore the attraction, the vulnerability she experienced around him. When he left, it would all fade.

From the corner of her eye she saw him standing, watching her. As she became involved in the game, it was several minutes before she looked again. He was gone. She wondered again why he'd come; he hadn't even tried to talk to her. Had he come just to watch her, see what she was doing? She pushed the thought away as the competition of the game claimed her attention again. She'd worry about Michael Donovan later. Given time he'd leave. Business would call and he'd return to Boston. Who knew when he'd find the time to leave again.

For one brief moment, Katie wished that were not the case; but she knew her husband.

The next morning Katie paused before Michael's door, indecision plaguing her. Was he inside? If so, should she just go on about her work, trying to ignore him, or come back later and hope he'd left for the morning? Behind the door she could hear the muted murmur of his voice. He was there. With firm resolution, she pushed the cart to the far end of the hall. She'd start here and hope he left before she reached his room.

Several hours later, Katie could no longer put it off. She'd taken care of all the rooms on her floor save Michael's. She knocked on the door. 'Housekeeping,' she called. There was no answer. Had he gone out? She crossed her fingers.

Opening the door with her passkey, her heart sank. Michael was sitting at the table near the large windows, his back to the door, talking on the phone. Katie kept her eyes on him as she slipped into the bathroom. He hadn't noticed her enter.

Going through the motions, she found herself strangely unsettled. Her heart was tripping in her chest, and her stomach felt as if butterflies had taken up permanent residency. What was wrong with her? She'd finish this room and go to the next floor. He probably wouldn't even know she was here. When Michael became caught up in business, he excluded everything else.

She could hear him as he discussed the situation with the person at the other end of the phone. His voice was calm and decisive. He knew how he wanted things done and was clear in informing those who worked for him.

When she moved to the bedroom, Katie was surprised when his eyes clashed with hers. She paused a moment, thinking he had been totally caught up with the conversation; she'd not expected him to turn around to see her. Her eyes widened slightly as she gazed into his. He didn't smile, or change expression in any way. Katie knew he was still listening to the other person on the phone, but his gaze bored into her. Breaking contact was almost physical, but she pulled away and went to make the bed. The background discussion of cubic feet of concrete, sky-cranes and Cat graders was a familiar litany. She'd heard Michael discuss such issues many, many times over the years.

She dusted the bedside table and looked over at the table where Michael sat. There were files and papers scattered all over. She couldn't dust it. Good, she didn't want to have to stay any longer than she must.

As she walked back to the door to get the vacuum cleaner, Michael's hand reached out and grabbed hers. Slowly, his eyes on her, he drew her to him until she stood up against his knees. His hand was gentle against her wrist, his thumb rubbing lazy circles against the delicate skin. Katie could scarcely breathe.

'Hold on, Steve.' He put the phone against his chest. 'Done so soon?' he asked, his voice gentle, his thumb the only reality Katie could focus on.

She nodded. 'Except for the vacuuming.'

'Leave that for now. I couldn't hear on the phone. Come back later and do it.'

'Call when you're ready.' She tugged at her hand, but his grip tightened.

'Are you going to play volleyball today?' he asked.

'No, not today.'

'Come out with me after you finish work.'

'No, I can't. I have plans.' Plans to stay as far away from this disturbing man as she could. 'I have to go.' She tugged at her hand again, fighting the old longings and sensations his touch wrought, fighting the lassitude and delight she felt.

He brought her wrist to his mouth and lightly touched it with his lips, releasing her hand, watching her closely the entire time.

Katie didn't wait, but fled as if he were chasing her. As she pulled the door shut behind her, she could hear him on the phone again. Always business.

She waited all afternoon for the call to finish the room. Waited with anticipation and dread. But the call never came.

When Katie left work, she had mixed emotions. Had she actually wanted to see Michael again? Shouldn't she feel glad he hadn't called?

3

Katie had the next day off, and she planned to avoid the hotel, the shops and the beach. If she could hold out long enough, she knew Michael would be gone. He was never absent from his business for long—a day here and there, but never any extensive time. Funny, they'd never taken a trip together. He'd been too caught up to take time for something as frivolous as a vacation.

The air was warm and soft against her cheeks as she went for her usual morning swim. Katie paused at the road's edge, scanning the beach for any runners. When she saw Michael in the distance, she sank down behind a sturdy palm, hidden in the early morning shadows. She was not up to a meeting with him today.

Once he had passed, she quickly went for her swim. Her usual pleasure in the morning ritual was dimmed as she kept a wary eye out in case he returned. She swam for a shorter time than she usually did, soon returning to her apartment with plans for chores that would keep her busy all day.

Katie wondered how long Michael planned to handle work long distance. Surely his business would be suffering if he wasn't there? At least, that was always the impression she got from him—that the world of Donovan Construction was nothing without its founder.

In the late afternoon, the phone rang. It was her friend Debbie from work. 'We're going to Mallory Square Dock later to watch the tourists watch the sunset, then have a cook-out at the beach. Want to come?'

'Sure do; what should I bring?' Katie welcomed the plan. It would get her out of the house and offer an alternative to the thoughts that kept spinning in her head.

'How about chips and some drinks. Meet you at the dock about five-thirty.'

Katie hung up the phone smiling. Viewing the sunset from Mallory Square Dock in Old Town was considered a very touristy thing to do, but she secretly loved it. She never admitted it to her friends because she didn't want to be teased, but she wandered that way several times each week to watch the spectacular sunsets over the Gulf.

Mallory Square was at the westernmost point of the island. From there everyone had a view of the sun as it appeared to drown in the deep blue of the Gulf of Mexico, flinging vibrant colors into the sky each evening, from bright coral to pale pink, blurring to teal and finally the dark violet that gave way to the black of the tropical night.

Evening picnics at the beach were also fun. Katie had been to three or four since she'd arrived, and she always enjoyed them. While the nights were cooler than the hot days, a fire was not strictly needed. Yet everyone enjoyed it when it was made. The flames danced in the darkness. The soft rhythm of the Gulf lapping the shore and the murmur of conversation made the picnics memorable.

She was not the first one to the rendezvous spot- Debbie, Marlise and several others she knew were already there, all wearing casual attire, shorts and loose shirts. It was still warm, the last rays of the sun refusing to let the air cool.

'Hi. Who else is coming?' She smiled at her new friends. They were accepting and easy to get along with. None of them wanted anything from her but her company. Katie loved spending time with them. Especially tonight—she'd been feeling cooped up in her apartment. Having spent most of her free time outdoors since arriving in Key West, she hadn't liked being inside all day. Yet that was the only way she could insure not running into Michael.

'Usual crowd. The tourist turnout is good.' Rick, Debbie's special friend, motioned to the large number of people along the road sitting on the beaches and in the small pavement cafes that crowded Mallory Square. Many more sat on the edge of the dock, feet dangling over the sea, eyes west. An air of festivity permeated the area as jugglers, mimes and other entertainers mingled with the crowd. The people were in high spirits, happily awaiting the daily event.

Katie recognized one tourist and turned swiftly away, hoping he hadn't seen her. But she reckoned without her friends. Marlise also recognized him and waved. 'He's a guest at the hotel,' she told the others.

Katie pretended she hadn't heard, her eyes firmly on the water before her.

'I think he's coming over,' Marlise announced.

'Oh, no, I don't think...' Katie turned, stricken. Before she could complete her sentence, however, Michael strolled over, his eyes smiling sardonically at Katie when he saw her expression.

She met his look and glanced away. She had spent all day avoiding him, avoiding thinking about him, or trying to at least, and now Marlise had brought him over. Was she never to be free of him?

'Good evening.' He smiled at everyone, his eyes coming back to Katie, flicking down to her mouth, back to her eyes.

Instantly she was reminded of their recent kiss. Angry with herself, she turned so she couldn't see him.

'Are you enjoying your visit?' Marlise asked. Naturally friendly, she took to heart the hotel's directive that employees do all they could to make the guests' stay a happy one.

'I'm at a bit of a loose end, but I am enjoying the island,' Michael replied, his eyes on Katie.

Introductions were made, then Marlise said, 'We're watching the sunset then going to a cook-out on the beach; care to join us?' She kindly did not admit they'd come to watch the tourists.

Katie threw her a dark look. 'I'm sure Mr. Donovan has already made plans for this evening.' She looked at him, trying to compel him to agree with her. But he shook his head.

'Actually, I had nothing planned.' His lips twitched as if he was amused at Katie's attempts to exclude him.

Katie looked away, defeated. Michael had never been at a loose end in his life; he always had his next step planned. But for some reason he wanted to accompany them. Why?

'Then please join us,' Debbie added.

Katie stared at the water, her eyes looking at the tourists, at the boats near by—anywhere but at Michael Donovan. He moved until he stood beside her, talking with Debbie and Marlise and Rick. When Jim joined them, he and Michael began a conversation about banking. Jim explained with great enthusiasm a deal he had recently completed for his firm, then launched into an explanation of a complex deal he was now negotiating. He was proud of its magnitude and was obviously trying to impress Michael.

Katie glanced briefly at him and her husband. What would Jim think if he knew the high sums of money Michael was used to dealing with? He would be stunned, and feel foolish. Michael, however, courteously listened to his discourse and made appropriate comments. She was glad, and touched by the sensitivity displayed by her husband. Why had she thought him totally ruthless? With a few brief words he could shatter Jim's illusions. Yet he refrained. Jim was nice, if young, and she was glad Michael hadn't deprecated any of his accomplishments. She wondered if Michael would actually do anything to help her friend. She didn't feel she was in much of a position to ask. Maybe he'd volunteer.

Three other friends joined their group, each laden with bags of food. Michael eyed all the bags. 'Should I go and get something to contribute?' he asked.

What she really wanted was for him to go, full stop. Maybe she could send him to get something and leave before he returned? No, that would be too awful. But she did wish he'd leave.

'No need, we have plenty,' Marlise assured him.

Katie still refused to look at him, though she could feel his eyes on her.

As the sky went through its nightly display, she forgot her unease and let the beauty of nature's evening ritual delight her. Michael leaned over to speak softly, his hand on her shoulder, moving to stand close to her. 'I was told not to miss this and now I know why,' he murmured. 'I usually avoid tourist places, but this is well worth it. I'm glad I came. It's beautiful.'

She could feel the heat from his body, a tingling awareness from her shoulders to the very core of her being. Was it the tropical air, mystical and mysterious? Feelings long dormant bloomed in the erotic setting of the island, the magic of the place making her more aware of everything. Fighting a strange longing to lean back against him, she kept herself ramrod-straight, eyes on the sky.

Odd, the sunset was not something she would have thought he'd appreciate. His sentiments were so close to her own that she forgot her awkwardness.

'It is beautiful, isn't it? I love coming here, but don't tell the others—they'd laugh at me. It's considered a tourist thing. We really came to watch the tourists, but I love the sunsets.' Her voice was also low, for him only. She glanced up at him.

His dark eyes looked down into hers as he slowly smiled, his face close.

'Our secret,' he said softly.

Katie had to drag her eyes from his. Time seemed to slow to a crawl. She blinked and stared at the sky as it darkened. Her heart rate increased, and she felt as if her clothes constricted. She had no business sharing secrets with Michael at this late date. They were in the process of separating their lives, not making new memories together.

She darted a quick glance at him. He was quietly staring at the spectacular colors painting the sky, the long low wisps of clouds a foil for the fading light. His hand still rested on her shoulder, and warmth spread throughout her body; even her heart warmed at his touch. For a moment Katie felt perfectly in tune with the man at her side.

The picnic on the beach turned out to be fun despite Michael's presence. The men built a roaring driftwood fire on which everyone cooked their own hot dogs. The buns got a little burned, but no one cared. Soft drinks and beer flowed freely and the talk was amusing, full of laughter and high spirits. Michael held his own with the group, but gave very little information about his life. Katie didn't think it was noticeable to anyone but her; but she wondered briefly how the others would react if they knew who Michael was.

It was so different from the parties and social affairs they were used to attending. Katie marveled at Michael's participation. It had taken a couple of picnics for her to feel comfortable and at ease around the fun-loving, casual group, but Michael fit in as if he'd been doing this all his life.

A flicker of impatience brushed through her. She didn't want him fitting in. She wanted him to feel awkward and out of place, and leave. Return to Boston and leave her alone.

As the evening passed, they grew quieter, drawing back a little from the fire and separating into small groups. Katie moved back from the heat, sitting quietly, happily watching her friends. Michael came to stretch out on the sand beside her, in the shadows that flickered and changed as the wood burned.

Watching the blazing fire as Rick fed more driftwood to the greedy flame, Katie was content. She let the sand, still warm from the sun, trickle through her fingers. The soft breeze from the sea carried the warm air gently by. It was still balmy, and the breeze gave only hint of coolness.

'This is fun,' she said softly, her eyes on the flickering flames.

Michael was lying back on one elbow, his face in shadow, but Katie felt his eyes on her.

'It is. Do you do this often?'

She turned to see him, the flickering light illuminating part of his face, then leaving it in darkness.

'This is my third or fourth time ever. I never did something like this as a child. Imagine doing this in February. Boston is snowed in.'

He smiled. 'I didn't know you were so against our winters.'

'I don't think I knew it myself. It's wonderful here. I love it.'

He fell silent. The night was clear, and the others around the fire talked softly among themselves or just stared into the flames.

'Have dinner with me tomorrow, Katherine? We can find a quiet restaurant with a secluded table—just the two of us,' Michael suggested. 'We still have to talk— we resolved nothing the other night.'

She started in surprise, wary of his motives.

'I don't really have anything dressy to wear, Michael. The

dress I wore the other evening is the only one I have, and it's not very dressy.'

'Is that the one you didn't wear a bra beneath?'

She smiled saucily over to him. 'It is. Do you have a problem with my not wearing a bra?' she asked, amusement evident in her tone.

'I find it damned distracting—as I imagine every other male within eyesight does.'

Katie chuckled softly. 'Hardly every male in sight.'

With a muffled oath, he reached out and pulled her to him, pushing her back on the sand and covering her mouth with his.

His kiss was wild and raw and hot. Her mouth was assaulted by the passion of his lips as he moved against her, demanding a response. The heat he generated permeated her whole body, spreading from her mouth to her breasts, to deep within her, until she was hot and feverish. Her senses spun, explosively caught up in emotions and feelings. The evening faded, the velvety night enclosing them so that Katie knew only the delight Michael wrought as his kiss went on.

His hands were hard on her shoulders, his chest pressing against her as if he wanted to meld their two bodies into one. Her breasts filled, throbbed, craved his touch. His lips moved and Katie responded. Her hands encircled his neck, pulling him closer, longing for his kiss to last forever.

The soft swish of the wind from the trees was lost in the blood pounding in her veins, and the warmth of the sand did not come close to the heat from Michael's body, the heat from his lips. Straining for completion, she moved against him, welcoming his weight as he lay across her, her hands caressing his back, feeling the strong muscles move beneath her fingers.

His mouth was moist, exciting. His tongue plunged deep within, dueled with hers, inviting it to invade his mouth. He sucked gently, and Katie's stomach lurched in reaction. The heat built up, and her lips responded, moving against his, her entire focus on their lips, mouths, tongues. His hand held her head as his assault spread fire to the far extremities of her limbs.

When he pulled back, Katie felt deserted. She noted that Michael was breathing hard, then with surprise that she was, too. She wished she could see his face, but the fire was behind him and he was in silhouette.

Slowly her hands fell to her side, and she stared up at the man she didn't know. Michael leaned over her for a few minutes as if he could see her face in the faint starlight, as if he was studying it, then he moved to sit up.

'Dinner?' His voice was normal, casual.

Katie felt shattered. She closed her eyes, feeling as if she'd completed a long roller-coaster ride—shaken and breathless. She hadn't been kissed like that in ages. Had she truly experienced the earth-shattering emotions churning within? Had he? How could he be so casual? Didn't he feel anything? Licking her lips, she tasted him again and her heart raced erratically.

Slowly she sat up, brushing sand from her hair, off her clothes. A quick glance to the others around the fire showed her that no one was looking their way, no one had seen anything. After such a momentous event, she was shocked that nobody had even noticed. That the world hadn't shifted.

Michael watched her, his face impassive, giving no clue to his thoughts or feelings. Katie knew that all the confusion she felt must be stamped clearly on her features. Did she want to have dinner with him? They were getting a divorce; why would he want to have dinner? If had anything to discuss, he could do so here.

'Katherine, don't analyze it, just say yes or no,' Michael's voice gently chided her.

She took a breath. 'I'll go to dinner.'

'I can pick you up at seven.'

'No, I'll come to the hotel.'

'Don't want me to see your place?' he guessed.

Katie found it hard to explain. It was her place, untouched by her past life. She had no memories with Michael there. And she was afraid to see him against that setting. Afraid she might always see him there, when she was trying to start over, without any reminders of him.

'Come to the hotel, then,' he told her.

She glanced at him. There had been understanding in his voice. Had he been aware of her feelings? She looked away. Not always—if he had, maybe she wouldn't want a divorce.

'I'll be there at seven. I'm going now.' She darted him a swift glance then looked away, her lips tingling. She longed for him to kiss her again. If he was as aware of her as she thought, he'd know.

He smiled a wicked smile, settling back in the sand. 'Goodnight, Katie. Maybe tomorrow night.'

Damn him, he did know, and was not going to kiss her again.

'You're mean,' she whispered. Daringly, without thinking, she reached over to brush her lips against his. She pulled back quickly, but not before she felt his response. Before he could do anything, however, she scrambled to her feet. Calling a goodnight to her friends, she ran lightly across the sand, heading for home running from the memory of his kiss, from the magical pull of attraction, from the man she'd once loved.

Try as she might, she couldn't outrun the memory. The scene replayed itself over and over. She didn't remember reaching out to Michael before. She'd been so in awe of him at first, then patterns and habits had taken hold and she was always the recipient of any touching.

Had Michael ever wanted her to initiate displays of affection? She was startled into stillness. No, he was a very assertive individual, as much in charge of his household as his business. If he'd wanted it different, he would have told her.

Still the thought stayed with her as she walked home.

It didn't become easier, she thought the next morning as she stood before his door. She didn't want to go in, yet knew she had to. Why didn't he go to the beach or the pool like ordinary tourists? Why come to this island paradise if he was just going to work all the time? He could do that in Boston.

She knocked and entered. As on the day before, Michael was on the phone. He ended the conversation, however, when he saw Katie, and hung up. Moving towards her, his expression was cautious.

'Good morning.' Her voice was steady.

'Good morning. We still on for tonight?'

She nodded.

'There's been a change. We can't do the quiet dinner I wanted. I have to attend a function in Miami. I want you to go with me.'

'You said last night dinner just for the two of us. What's this function in Miami?'

'A meeting with some Brazilians who are interested in a high-rise complex in the new capital. Donovan Construction has had the bid in for weeks, several of the principals are here on another matter, and it would be a perfect opportunity to meet with them and further our efforts for that contract.'

'You don't need me for that,' she said, hurt that once again business took precedence over everything else. She knew better, why did she even bother. Michael wasn't going to change.

'I do need you,' he insisted. 'Their wives are accompanying them. I want you to entertain them. Also show them I have a wife. They are particular about things like that.'

'You don't have a wife, Michael. We're getting a divorce.' She stepped back, trying to get away from him, trying to escape the trap that loomed before her.

'We're still married until the divorce is final. For heaven's sake, Katherine, you've done this kind of thing a thousand times before; what's one more night?'

'I don't want to go to Miami with you.'

He paused and turned to look out of the window. The silence stretched out for several long minutes. Katie watched him, knowing he was thinking of other ways to convince her. She'd seen him in action over the years, she knew what he was doing, but not what to expect.

'The hotel expects its employees to do all they can to ensure the guests are having a good time,' Michael began. 'I don't think asking you to go to dinner with me is such a big favor.'

'I don't think the hotel expects us to make sure you have that good a time,' she replied dryly.

He spun around to face her again. 'Dammit, Katherine, I'm not asking you to sleep with me, just go to dinner. You agreed last night to do so. We'll just go to Miami instead of staying here.'

She was silent a long time, trying to see the fallacy of his argument. Miami was a long way from Key West. She'd feel safer staying in Key West. She didn't want to go. But maybe it would put him in a good mood and they could talk on the drive back. She nodded slowly.

A hint of triumph gleamed in Michael's eyes as he smiled at her response.

'Fine. I'll get you at five—we need to meet them at eight and it's almost three hours' drive to Miami.'

'I'll be ready. Did you remember I only have the one sun dress that could be considered at all dressy?' Maybe he'd let her out of her agreement, knowing she wouldn't be suitably attired.

'I'll buy you one from the shop downstairs.'

'No.'

'Katherine, be reasonable; you can't impress these South Americans if you're dressed in a cotton sundress. I want to impress, show them how successful Donovan Construction is so they'll have confidence in the firm. If you had brought one of your dresses from home that I paid for, you would wear it. What's the difference?'

'The difference is that we are not married anymore. I can't accept an expensive dress from you.'

'We are married. Hell, wear it tonight and send it back to me—at least you'll look the part this evening.' His voice was dangerously low and calm.

Katie could feel the leashed energy as if it were a tangible thing. She tried to stare him down, but his eyes glittered down at her, his whole body poised as if to attack.

'Very well.' She conceded defeat. 'But not from the dress shop downstairs. Can you imagine the rumors that would fly? I work here, after all.'

He frowned, disliking to be reminded.

'Take my credit card and buy the dress wherever you like. I'll get you at five,' he said.

'I'll be downstairs then.' She moved stiffly into the bathroom to begin. She felt as if she were in a dream, one part of her going through the motions of her routine day, the other dwelling on the purchase she must make and the evening ahead.

Michael was on the phone again when she left the room.

The dress Katie bought was long white silk, with blue trim at the neck and hem. It lovingly followed the lines of her figure, dropping to a softly draped skirt that swayed seductively against her long legs as she walked. The neckline was deep and there were no sleeves. Her smooth, tanned skin was displayed to full advantage by the dress.

She felt the familiar resignation settle over her as she entered the lobby. She had done this so many times before, yet had grown more and more to resent it. She'd much rather stay home, with a good book, or a TV show to watch. But she was committed, and she'd do her best.

Michael was prompt stepping off the elevator at five and smiled when he saw her. His eyes ran down the length of her dress and Katie felt as if he'd touched her. She blushed and turned away, trying not to show her reaction.

'You look lovely,' he murmured as he drew close. Reaching to take her hand, he threaded his fingers through hers and led the way to the rental car. It was a Lincoln, spacious and luxurious. At home, they had a BMW and a Mercedes. Was he trying something new in Florida?

As they headed north on Highway One, over the long causeways and the other islands of the Keys, Michael told her about the prospects he was entertaining that evening. He revealed the terms of the contract proposed and what he wanted to accomplish during the visit, keeping the conversation firmly on business.

It was just before eight when they reached the opulent Royal Miami Hotel, right on Miami Beach. Evening had darkened the sky, but the bright lights glittering from the row of hotels lit up the night and cloaked the beach in enchantment.

'I've arranged a small reception, with dinner afterwards. There will be others besides the South American contingent,' he'd said earlier, so Katie knew what to expect when they reached the portico.

The evening was like many others she'd spent with Michael—talking to his guests, making people feel comfortable, introducing strangers to each other, and circulating to make sure everyone had what he or she wanted. Katie handled it perfectly. Only she was aware that she didn't wish to be there. This was the life she'd forsaken months ago.

As the evening passed, her anger grew, at herself, and at Michael. She should never have agreed to come. She'd known exactly what the evening would be like. She was a gracious hostess, doing her best to make the others attending the affair comfortable and happy.

She was bored.

Glancing at her watch, she frowned. It was after midnight already, and it would take three hours to get back to Key West. A touch of suspicion had her seeking Michael. It was getting very late; was he going to be able to drive to Key West? They should have left before now. She had to work in the morning. At this rate, she'd get a nap instead of a good night's sleep.

Spotting him with the Brazilians, she threaded her way through the crowd and tried to get his attention. He had another drink in his hand. How many had he had during the evening? Too many to drive? Wariness crept into her.

Smiling genially at the guests, she touched Michael on his arm. 'Don't you think we should be going?' she said softly, trying to convey her message with her eyes.

'It's early yet. Have you met Senor Fresco? He's visited Key West and we were discussing the best seafood restaurant on the island.'

His arm came to rest on her shoulders, his fingers slowly caressing her neck. Katie tried to follow the discussion with Senor Fresco, but was too aware of Michael's hand on her skin, the fluttering of her heart at his touch, the quivering felt deep inside at the slow fondling of his fingers. She could concentrate on nothing beside Michael, sheltering her as she stood in the protection of his arm, his fingers flooding her body with desire and yearning. She could only stare at the others in their group as the conversation swirled about her. Michael consumed her.

At long last the evening drew to a close. Katie's face felt tired from smiling so much. She bid the last guest goodnight and glanced at her watch, horrified to see it was after two. They couldn't get home before dawn. She stormed her way across the room to Michael. Anger at the situation, anger at her reaction to him flooded through her; she was ready to explode.

'Michael, are you planning to drive us home now?'

He looked at her and then his watch. 'It's late, Katherine, I'm tired. We can get a nap here before starting back.'

'I don't want to stay here; I want to go back now.'

'Be reasonable; it's almost three o'clock in the morning. I've been up all day and you know that drive is monotonous. I couldn't stay awake. It's too dangerous.'

'So we just get a room here, I suppose?' Her voice wobbled slightly. She was furious at herself for being talked into coming. She should have guessed the dinner would last far longer than a couple of hours. Now she was stuck in Miami until Michael decided to drive them back.

'I—uh—did book a room for us,' he said quietly, taking her arm in his firm grasp.

'One room?' She didn't know whether to throw a fit or not. What was he doing?

'It was all they had available on such short notice.''

He escorted her to the elevator. When it arrived, Michael pressed the number for their floor. Another couple stepped in, pressed for the floor above them. Silence reigned in the small car as it rose quietly to the floors indicated. The doors opened and

Michael gently propelled Katie out to the hall.

'Did you plan this?' she asked in a tight voice as they walked to the room Michael had reserved.

'I thought we might be late, if that's what you mean.' He opened the door, only releasing her arm once they were inside with the door shut behind them.

'I'm not staying the night with you.' She stalked over to the window; it overlooked the Atlantic Ocean, only a dark expanse at night. In the morning the view would be lovely.

She turned back to look at him and was startled to see a small overnight case on the stand near the bed.

'You did plan this. You even brought a suitcase. I'm not staying.' She stomped over to the door, but Michael hadn't moved. He gripped her shoulders with his hard hands.

'Katherine, stop right now and listen to me. I am not planning a seduction scene. I'm tired and want to sleep for a few hours before driving that long causeway back to Key West. I brought a change of clothes. That's all.'

He shook her slightly and let her go, his hands slowly releasing her.

'It's not all. Michael, I have a job to get to. I have to be at work at seven. If you sleep for a while, it'll be long after seven getting back, and I'll still be in the clothes I left in last night. I can't believe you're doing this to me. Are you trying to get me fired? To ruin my reputation in Key West? Have you no consideration?'

'You wouldn't have to worry about a job or your reputation if you'd give up this silly idea and come back home.' His voice was hard.

'I won't give up the idea and I won't be coerced into it by your shabby tactics,' she retorted.

He rubbed his eyes with one hand, moving to stand by the

window. He gazed out for a long time, then sighed gently and turned to face her.

'I apologize, Katherine; I hadn't thought about it from your point of view. Of course I don't want to coerce you into anything, or make things difficult for you. I'll get us back to Key West before you're due to start work.'

She stared at him in surprise. She had not expected him to see her side of it, or apologize. But it was the first time she could remember when she'd stood up for herself. Maybe she should have done it before.

Michael turned to look at her. 'Get some sleep. I'll arrange a charter flight to Key West to get us there before you start work.'

He left the room, leaving Katie standing in the middle, surprised at the turn of events.

4

They arrived back in Key West with enough time for Katie to shower and change. She sent the silk dress to the cleaners with instructions to have it delivered to Michael when it was ready. She'd spoken very little to him on the flight back to Key West, only wishing to end their trip and return to her normal pursuits.

When she changed into her uniform for her shift, she approached her friend Debbie.

'Would you change floors with me?' Katie asked. 'The man in 1121 has asked me out a couple of times and it's a little awkward now.' It sounded weak to her.

But Debbie smiled and nodded. 'Sure, no problem. I'd feel funny, too, cleaning someone's room that I knew. Just let me know when you want to switch back.'

With Debbie taking her floor, Katie had no worries about running into Michael during her shift. She breezed through her work, contemplating the early evening she was going to have to make up for being up so late the night before. She refused to let herself think about the dinner, or the ride home on the small plane. The sooner Michael left, the better she'd be.

Katie had cleaned all her rooms and was ready to change from her uniform when Mrs. Dowling, the head of housekeeping, popped her head in the locker-room.

'There you are, Katie; would you take some towels up to room 1121? The guest there said he'd like some more. Isn't that one of your rooms?'

Katie nodded, not wanting to tell her boss why she and Debbie had switched. Gathering a stack of towels, she headed quickly for the service elevator.

Knocking on the door, she waited. What did he want now?

The door opened and he smiled at her. For a second Katie's heart stopped, then sped up. She stared back at him for endless minutes, forgetting where she was, why she'd come.

'The towels—thanks.' He drew her into the room. 'Why didn't you clean the room today?' he asked.

She turned and placed the towels on the counter in the bathroom, preparing to leave. But he blocked the door.

'We—um—rotate rooms. It's Debbie who has this floor now,' she prevaricated.

'I'm sorry about last night, Katherine. Thank you for going with me, and helping me out. I think we'll get the deal.'

'I'm glad for you, Michael. If you'd let me out, I'd like to go home. I'm tired and my shift is over now.'

'Have dinner with me?'

'No.' She tried to reach the door, but he stood firmly in the way.

'Tomorrow night, then. The quiet restaurant for just the two of us, for our talk. You said yes on the beach.'

She stared at him. She didn't want to see him again. She was tired of the constant need to be on her guard, to fight her feelings and the attraction he held for her. She'd made up her mind months ago that their marriage was over. They should have had their talk on the long ride to Miami.

'Not in Miami.' She would go out with him one last time and make him understand they were finished.

'Fine; tomorrow night at seven o'clock. We'll try that sea-food restaurant Senor Fresco recommended.'

Katie worried all the next day about dinner, with mixed emotions, looking forward to it on one hand, yet worried she was making a mistake on the other. She wanted to end her relationship with Michael, and didn't see how dining together worked towards that end. He said he wanted to talk with her, but couldn't he have talked on the long drive to Miami? Her one attempt to broach the subject had resulted in a quick change of topic.

Katie dressed with extra care that evening. It could be her last dinner with Michael. She thought back to the many meals they had shared with friends or businessmen. It was hard to remember when just the two of them had eaten casually—made do. Even if they'd not had a party, the meals they'd shared had been formal, with Frances serving and clearing. The conversation had been superficial and meaningless.

There was nothing left to say, why prolong the situation?

She brushed her hair until it shone, the curls lightened by the sun. Her tan was deep, her eyes brown and sparkling. She viewed herself in the mirror, his comments from the picnic springing to mind.

She jerked away from the mirror. She wasn't out to entice the man. She grabbed her sweater in case it was cool inside the restaurant. She didn't need air-conditioning if her windows were open, but the public buildings ran it for the tourists.

Promptly at seven she rapped on his door.

He opened it, immaculately dressed in a crisp white shirt, lightweight navy suit and bold red tie. For a second Katie regretted leaving the pretty dresses in Boston, and returning the silk dress.

She lifted her chin. So her dress was casual—it suited her new lifestyle. Anyway, she was not out to impress anyone. Only to have dinner, have their talk, say goodbye and get on with life.

'I assume we can walk?' Michael said as he joined her in the hall. 'Everything seems close together here.'

'We either walk or ride bikes,' she murmured. 'No real need for cars.' But she knew Debbie's friend Rick would disagree—his taxi service depended on tourists riding instead of walking.

Michael was silent as they walked the dozen blocks to the Fresh Catch, mingling with others on their way to dinner. The streets were filled with happy tourists enjoying the pleasures of the island.

Katie had never eaten there, but she recognized the type immediately upon entering. The maitre d' was suave, seating them quickly in a small alcove. The linen was starched, snowy white, the place setting of elegant heavy silver. The lighting was dim, with scented candles on every table. It was expensive, but the food and service would be worth it.

'Quite a change from Marco's, where we had pizza,' she said, smiling politely at Michael as they were seated.

'And which do you prefer, Katherine?' he asked, his eyes boring into her as he awaited her response. Her own eyes flickered around the room before meeting his.

'This is nice, Michael, but I love Marco's. I'm afraid it's very plebeian of me, but I find I like the more common things—fast-food places, inexpensive shops and activities. Maybe it's the novelty. I've found some friends and am happy learning what I like to do, the different kinds of people I like to be around and the accomplishments I have.'

'So different from our life in Boston?'

'Yes.' Deliberately so.

She picked up the menu and perused it, trying to ignore his

stare. She felt as if he were touching her, so strong was the pull. The words blurred before her eyes, meaningless. There was only Michael, sitting across from her, gazing at her lowered head.

His hand reached across and took the menu from her unresisting fingers.

'Want shrimp?' he asked gently.

She looked up, about to nod and let him order for her as she had every time before, when she remembered.

'No, thanks. I'll order my own dinner when the waiter comes.' She bravely met his eyes and remembered her last evening in Boston. She'd stood up to him then, and he'd ignored her. Refused to take her seriously. She'd had to walk out to prove her point. What would he do tonight?

'Liberated,' he murmured and turned to look at his menu.

Katie ordered her own meal—swordfish, while Michael ordered shrimp. They had wine while they waited.

'Now, do you want to talk, Michael?' she asked, as the silence stretched out too long.

'I don't want this divorce, Katherine. I want you to come back to Boston. Or we can take that cruise I spoke of—you tell me what you want. But let's try to work things out.'

'I don't want to work anything out. I like what I'm doing now,' she said gently.

'You don't miss me at all?'

She looked up at the tone in his voice. His eyes were on his wine; his jaw clenched tightly, his knuckles white as he gripped the glass stem. His face was impassive. Did he care either way? Or was he only angry because he could not dictate the outcome?

He was so good-looking that her heart almost stopped. His face was leaner now, but strong and assertive. The bronze he'd acquired in the last couple of days only added to his good looks.

To her eye he looked alert and dangerous. He hadn't made a fortune in a tough business like construction by being a pushover. He had an air of ruthlessness about him, and it showed in the way he ran his life.

But for a moment, a second, Katie thought she heard hurt in his tone. She sighed and shook her head.

'Michael, you and I were wed, but we didn't have a marriage. Marriage is a sharing of two lives. We lived side by side in a great house, meeting for meals. You directed everything, orchestrated all our activities. And they were all aimed at advancing Donovan Construction. But you didn't share your life with me, nor share mine. There's very little to miss.'

He looked up at her, his eyes dark, impassive, and, coolly lifting one eyebrow, he watched her in the muted light.

'And what are you looking for from life, Katherine? Some man who has nothing, but will devote his every moment to you? You'd get tired of that fast.'

She thought briefly of Rick and Debbie. They had little money, but a lot of love and happy times together. They liked their life, didn't wish for it to be any different.

'I would hope I wouldn't have money problems, but if my wants are modest I shouldn't. I manage now on my own salary, and it certainly isn't much. There's more to life than buying things, or going on expensive trips. You enjoyed the picnic on the beach, didn't you?'

He nodded.

'It cost virtually nothing.'

The salad arrived and for a few moments talk was suspended.

'Are you planning to remarry?' Michael asked, his voice tight, his eyes on his food.

'I don't know. If I meet the right man,' she said. 'I'd like to have some kids.'

He looked up, startled. 'I never knew that.'

'You never asked,' she said simply, meeting his eyes.

He was silent, brooding. 'I don't like the idea of anyone else touching you.'

Katie's lips tightened. He was being possessive, as if she were a crystal vase that no one should touch. She was her own person, no longer his concern, and he needed to know that.

'It's no longer your business, Michael. I'll let whomever I wish touch me.' Her eyes flashed brown fire as she challenged him.

His were dark, almost black in his face.

'We'll just see about that. Damn it, Katherine, I want you home.'

'I am home, and, the sooner you accept that, the better off we'll both be,' she hissed back, conscious of the other diners, of some of the looks being cast their way. She didn't want to make a scene. She'd leave first.

Michael glanced around, then took a deep breath.

'Tell me about living here,' he said, his voice neutral, his anger of a moment ago gone, or at least leashed so that she didn't hear it.

Slowly at first, watching to see if he was bored, then with more enthusiasm, Katie described her experiences since arriving at the small island—finding a job, furnishing her apartment. She continued after the entree was served.

'I love the climate. It's so different; I can almost touch the air—it's soft and always scented with the sea, unless it's scented with some of the flowers that grow around here, like the frangipani and jasmine. Quite different from the smoggy, damp smell we sometimes got in Boston.'

'So you'd forsake New England for the south.'

'Everything moves at a slower pace here, people seem to

care more about each other, or maybe it's the people themselves. I didn't meet any like that in Boston. People I knew there were constantly trying to prove how much money they had, or how much influence they carried. No one seemed to care about anyone else.'

'Several of your committee members have asked after you since you've been gone,' Michael murmured.

'Me, or Michael Donovan's wife?' She glared at him. 'When I'm finished work here, I do whatever I wish. I'm not always working, as you are, Michael. I've discovered snorkeling, diving, and volleyball. I like going to the movies, or just hanging out with my friends.'

Unruffled, he filled her wine glass again, and encouraged her to continue telling him about Key West. He asked her questions, seemed interested in everything she had to say.

When Michael paid the bill, Katie watched him curiously. He was relaxed, at ease in surroundings familiar to him, to them both. He was at home in the expensive restaurant as he had been at the pizza place. Had he always had the ability to fit into wherever he was? She always pictured him at work in the high-rise glass and concrete building that dominated downtown Boston; and at the expensive nightclubs and restaurants they had frequented in the name of work. Yet she knew he visited the construction sites, talked to the men working the jobs. Had he talked to them as equals?

When he helped her from her chair, she swayed slightly.

'Oops, too much wine,' she said, standing still for a moment to get her equilibrium back.

He drew her hand through the crook of his arm and let his hand remain on hers. It was hard, warm, callused, and caused the most peculiar sensations to race down her skin. She looked up at him with her eyes wide, a question clearly within them.

'Come back to my room with me and we'll finish our discussion,' he said as they walked from the restaurant.

'I shouldn't. I need to get home and to bed. I have to work early in the morning.' Her head was delightfully light, and she seemed to float as they walked along.

'You have time for a nightcap. I don't want to stop now. Katherine, I want you to consider everything and see if we can take one more chance. I'll cut back on work; devote more time to you. We'll do things differently, decide what we both want to do and do that. Think it over; don't decide tonight.'

She felt as if she were gliding along, floating on air. Her only anchor was the strength in his arm. Her fingers were gripping as if she didn't want to let go. She enjoyed the feel of his hand covering hers. It must be the wine.

Was it imprudent to return with him to his room? What if he tried to make love to her? Her heart sped up with the thought. What if he did? She remembered his kisses on the beach, and heat washed through her body. Why did his lovemaking seem different here in Key West, more exciting? Was there special magic in the tropical night not found in colder climes?

They were still married; if he changed a little, would she want to stay married? She glanced at him from under her lashes. He didn't seem the same as the ruthless, hard-working businessman from Boston she knew so well.

He was mysterious, exciting, intriguing. Was it the spell of the islands? Or had Michael somehow changed? Had she changed?

She was still musing over these things when he unlocked the door to his room, and drew her inside. It was dark when he shut the door behind them, but he had no difficulty finding her, finding her mouth and covering it with his own.

His lips were hot and demanding, seeking to arouse, to entice and to conquer. His arms came around her and drew her tightly against him, her body pressed against the length of his. His hands moved in delectable patterns against her spine, his long legs braced to support them. His mouth plundered the sweetness of hers.

Katie's head began to spin, and her breathing grew uneven. His lips moved, and again his kiss was wild and hot. She could scarcely breathe, scarcely think, only feel the floating euphoria of his touch.

His hand moved to cup one breast, teasing her nipple to awareness through the thin fabric of her dress. Igniting a fire within her that grew with each passing second, his touch electrified her, her senses raced, as currents of delight flashed through her.

He tilted her head and trailed hot, fiery kisses along her throat to the smooth tops of her shoulders, hot kisses that warmed her, inflamed her and made her ache with longing for more—more of his touch, more of his kisses, all over her skin.

She reached up and slipped his jacket from his shoulders letting it fall on the floor. Moving against him to feel his muscles beneath her hands, to feel the hard wall of his chest against the softness of her breasts crushed against him, she was consumed with the passion that filled the room.

Where had this passionate man come from? Where had she hidden her passion all these years? She wanted to rip the clothes from his body, have him do the same to her and carry her to the bed, or just sink on to the floor.

The strident ring of the phone shattered the dark night. It penetrated the fog-cloud in Katie's mind and she pulled back, her eyes wide in horror at what was happening. At what had almost happened. She stepped back as Michael released her.

He flicked on the light and strode to the phone. Numbly she watched him, blinking in the lighted room.

'Donovan... Yeah, Steve, what's up...?'

Katie watched as the minutes ticked by, as Michael became caught up in the work problem being discussed on the phone, as he forgot her presence entirely.

So much for his talk of changing. He couldn't even keep away from business for one evening.

She looked at the clock. It was after ten-thirty and still they called him. Did none of them sleep? Was business all-consuming for all of them? It always had been for Michael. He filled his days and most of his evenings with work, as if he had no other life apart from it.

Quietly, slowly, she moved to the door, eased it open and slipped through. She ignored the tiny ache in her heart. It was the same old story; why had she thought it would be different at all? The wine had muddled her senses; she knew this man, knew how he thought, how he worked.

He never saw her go.

Katie did not take her morning swim the next day. She stayed in the privacy of her apartment and tried to read the paper. The scenes from last night replayed, however, and she couldn't concentrate. She saw herself in Michael's arms, reveling in his kiss, his touch, and longing for more, regretting the interruption of the phone.

Squirming in her chair, she chided herself for being disturbed by memories she'd do best to forget.

Sure, he'd devoted himself to her, drawn her out at dinner, evidenced a desire for her company—almost convinced her he'd change, that business would not come before her. Until the reality of his business took hold. When business called, everything else was dropped—it commanded his immediate and complete attention.

She was furious with herself for even considering for one second changing her mind about their separation. She had spent years with the man; she knew how he was. He'd do anything to get his way, then move on to the next challenge. Promise her the moon until she was safely ensconced in Boston, then move on to the next problem.

He'd seen her leaving as a challenge: bring her round, satisfy his longing for domination, then he'd start on something else, content to let her live as she had been doing for the last several years.

Thank goodness for the phone call—it had saved her from making a fool of herself. She had almost been convinced, almost persuaded. It must have been the wine. She'd guard against it in the future, and against him.

She rode her bike to work, enjoying the bright colors along the route, the air still cool and soft after the balmy night. The stalls of colorful T-shirts, straw hats and souvenirs were just opening. It was too early for the tourists. Only a few people were on the streets.

When she pushed her cart off on to her floor, Katie was startled to find Michael waiting by the elevator door.

'Good morning, Katherine.' His voice was quiet. He pushed away from the wall and moved closer.

'What are you doing here?' she asked, pushing the bulky cart down towards the first room.

'You left very abruptly last night.'

She paused and looked up at him. 'Michael, we had dinner, had our talk. I have not changed my mind. And you haven't changed either. The minute something from work crops up, you're on it.'

'If that's all--'

'No, it's not. It was the whole way of life we lived. I want more than to be a figurehead at some charity. I want to do things, share with people, feel more alive. I want children, a family, traditions started. I have to go to work now. And when I'm finished I'll do something totally different, like go swimming, or snorkeling, or shopping—I won't spend eight hours here and then do the same thing for the rest of my waking hours the way you do. Goodbye, Michael.'

He remained standing while she pushed her cart towards the first door. Knocking, and entering, Katie began work.

Quickly and efficiently going about her tasks, she finished early. She had no further encounters with Michael. Not wanting to linger to chat with any of the others, she changed and left as soon as she could.

Avoiding any place that could conceivably find Michael Donovan for the next two days, Katie was a virtual recluse. She avoided her usual haunts, did not go to the beach, nor through the main streets of town. She wasn't sure she could trust herself if she ran into Michael.

On the third morning, Debbie was at work before Katie. 'Hey, Katie, haven't seen you for a while.'

She smiled her greeting, changing into her uniform.

'Been busy?'

Katie nodded, beginning to change from her shorts.

'Want to change floors back now that the delectable Mr. Donovan's gone? Or just stay the way we are? Doesn't matter to me.'

'Michael's gone?' Katie looked at Debbie, startled.

He'd gone. And she hadn't known it; he hadn't even said goodbye. She sat down on the bench, her legs weak. He'd finally gone. Why wasn't she happier?

'A day or so ago. Didn't you know?'

'No, I—er—I hadn't seen him for a while. Just a friend–' She trailed off, rising to finish dressing slowly. She should be feeling relieved that he'd left. That was what she'd wanted. She knew they had no future together, and she didn't need him here causing trouble for her. Only she would have thought he'd say goodbye.

'I thought you looked like more than friends; there was a certain spark—I don't know, as if you could be more than friends, especially at the picnic we had on the beach,' Debbie said, sitting on the bench ready for a long chat.

'No, our worlds are too different. Michael's a businessman, rich, successful, and quite caught up in it.' Katie's voice was slightly muffled as she pulled her dress on. Had Debbie seen his kiss at the picnic?

'Must be doing all right to afford to stay at this place. Oh, well, not for the likes of us working gals.' Debbie rose. 'Not that I'd trade Rick for anyone. But somehow I thought you and Michael suited each other. Listen, we're going out to the movies tonight—Marlise, too. Want to come?'

'Sure, what's playing?'

They grabbed their carts, nodded to the other women just coming in, and headed for the elevator, discussing the relative merits of the films playing at the local theater. Key West was small, so there were not a lot of choices when it came to movies.

Katie felt split in two. Part of her was with Debbie, listening, murmuring something when appropriate; the rest of her was dwelling on the fact that Michael had left, and the void that opened in her life.

This was what she wanted. He must have finally realized she meant what she said, and given up. Maybe leaving him the other night had shown him at last that she was serious. They'd had their talk; it changed nothing. There was no more to be said.

5

Katie continued to enjoy spending time with her friends, continued to try to decide what she wanted to do with her future, and swam in the ocean every day. Some of the initial sparkle faded, however. It became more of an effort to do some things, to feel the enthusiasm she had once felt. She refused to speculate on why that was.

When they had another nighttime picnic, she remembered Michael and the passionate kiss he'd given her. When she rode her bike downtown, she'd pass the Fresh Catch restaurant and remember their last dinner, and what had almost happened afterwards. When she'd hear a small plane circle overhead, she'd remember their return from Miami. Even working on a different floor was a reminder of Michael.

She continued to do the rooms that had been Debbie's. She didn't want to go into 1121, didn't want to remember Michael's presence there, or that final night. She was content to stay on the lower floor.

She wished he'd never come, had never left his impression on Key West, had left it solely hers. But he had, and it was up to her to forget him. Forget the few magic kisses, the warmth seeing him had brought, she told herself. She was curiously saddened by his leaving, but it was what she wanted. Forget him and move on.

February ended and March began. It didn't seem as though the number of tourists remained high as spring approached. When Katie asked Debbie if she was imagining it, Debbie said it was true.

'Soon they'll taper off and it'll be quiet for a week or two. Then over Easter we're swamped with obnoxious college kids. They don't usually stay here, of course- it's too expensive—but they're everywhere else on the island.'

'If it's so awful, why does the town let them come?'

'Lots of money. You can put up with a lot of things for the money they bring in during a three-week period.'

'Like Fort Lauderdale,' Katie said, remembering the stories she'd read in years past.

'Exactly, only without as much publicity. Want to go for a Coke?'

'Sure, just let me finish up here.' Katie cleaned up her cart, changed her clothes and left with her friend, wondering what changes she'd see with the arrival of the college kids. She wanted to experience Key West in all its phases. Winter had been ideal, with flowers in bloom, and the weather constantly warm and sunny. She hoped the rest of the seasons were as delightful.

Though whether she'd stay in Key West remained to be seen. She didn't want to work in a hotel all her life. She spent endless hours trying to decide exactly what she wanted to do. But for the time being she was content to glide along, enjoying herself, and saving a little money. There would be time enough to find another job, start on a new career. She'd wait until the divorce was final, then decide.

Two days later, Katie left work alone and there he sat, on the curb by the employees' entrance, dressed in faded cut-offs, a baggy T-shirt and scuffed, dirty tennis shoes. Katie saw him immediately, paused and looked again to be sure. It was Michael Donovan.

He looked up at her when she approached and smiled lazily. Katie felt her heart turn over. A sudden happiness flooded her and she frowned, trying to hang on to sanity.

'Michael? Whatever are you doing here? And dressed like that?' He always dressed in quality men clothing.

'Hi, Kath—Katie.' He rose easily until he stood beside her. His face was pale compared to the natives, his tan of a few weeks ago faded. His attire, however, would blend in with the best of the beachcombers. She hadn't known he even owned such clothes.

'I've moved to Key West. Isn't this how the people dress here?'

'Yes, but...' The words penetrated. 'What do you mean you've moved here?'

He reached out and trailed his fingers down her cheek, down her neck, his eyes following his hand, avoiding her eyes. Katie shivered at his touch, her heart fluttering.

'I mean, you didn't like Boston, didn't like how we lived there, so I thought I'd try Key West. We'll try your way for a while.'

She blinked up at him, uncertainty giving way to a growing belief. 'You moved here, like in you're planning to live here permanently?'

'Hmm. I told you I didn't want to let you go.'

'That's the most ridiculous thing I've ever heard. You can't move here. This is nothing like Boston. How can you run your business from here? The only airline service is small planes. No multi-communications network, no international jets, no high-priced lawyers–'

He put his fingers over her mouth, his own lips twitching as she fell silent.

'I put Steve in charge of Donovan Construction, gave Frances an early retirement, and closed the Boston house. I left most of my clothes there, bringing only what I thought I'd need here. I'm not going to work. You work; you can support us for a while.'

She stared at him, stunned. Shaking her head, she stepped back. 'You've gone crazy. Michael, I want a divorce. I don't want you living here.'

'And I think we should give our marriage a try again.' His voice was patient.

'No.' This was worse than when she'd tried to explain why she was leaving. He just wouldn't listen to her.

He sighed and looked around the small alley. 'Okay, then. I guess you're adamant. But I'm in a fix. I can't return immediately. I would look crazy then. I'll stay a while, return to Boston after the summer. At least I know a few people here—Rick, Debbie, Jim.' He turned back to her. 'You.'

She frowned, wanting to make him leave immediately, wanting him to stay away from her, from her friends. Looking at him suspiciously, she had a sudden thought. Michael didn't give up so easily; he always went after what he wanted with a single-minded determination. Why the sudden agreement?

'And the divorce—are the attorneys still working on it?' He hadn't stopped that, had he?

'Yes. I told them to hold off when I was here before, but if you are of the same mind I guess I'll have them wrap it up. It'll be a few more months, that's all.'

She nodded. When the silence began to stretch out awkwardly, she said, 'Well, see you.' She watched him for another minute, then turned and walked slowly away, towards home.

Emotions churning as she walked, Katie tried to analyze how she felt. She couldn't. All she could feel was the surprise that he'd returned, shock at what he'd proposed, and a small, small question of what it would be like if they tried it.

Determined to let Michael's return make no difference to her life on the island, Katie rose at her normal time and went for her swim. Michael was on the beach, lying on the sand not far from where she usually swam. She had halfway expected it. Why wasn't he running? She paused on the sand in indecision. Lifting her chin, determined not to be intimidated, she ignored him, walking out to the water's edge, discarding her shorts and top and plunging into the sea.

The water was heavenly. Still, soft, warm, it caressed her as she swam, its touch like silk against her skin. The sun's rays were hot even at this early hour, sparkling on the water, peeping over the tall palms that lined the beach. She enjoyed this quiet time each morning.

When she'd had enough, she turned for the shore, not surprised to find Michael had moved and was now lounging lazily back on the sand beside her towel and clothes, his eyes on her. He watched her as she swam in, stood and waded the rest of the way.

She felt the blood pound in her ears as she walked towards him, her wet swimsuit molding her figure like a second skin. Conscious of his eyes on her, boldly assessing her as she drew closer, she flushed and looked away, trying to pretend he wasn't there. But not succeeding. Every nerve ending was quivering with the touch of his eyes, every inch of her body felt as if he'd touched her, caressed her.

She snatched up her towel and held it as a defense against his look.

'Good morning.' He smiled up at her, his eyes indolently

roaming over her figure, laughing at her feeble attempts to hide her body from his gaze. Katie felt a little foolish, but kept the towel in place.

'Good morning.' Her greeting was grudgingly returned. When she ventured to look at him, he was staring out over the water. Dressed in the same cut-offs as yesterday, he had a sleeveless T-shirt on this morning, displaying pink skin on his shoulders and arms.

'Don't get burned. The sun can be fierce this time of year,' she said involuntarily as she saw the reddened skin.

He glanced up, then away; a smile touched his lips.

'Too late—I stayed out too long yesterday. I've got to stay inside today, I guess. What's there to do here, if you don't lie on the beach?'

'For tourists, there's Hemingway's place, the old lighthouse, or the Old Town Trolley Tours. Those should keep you out of the sun.'

'And sunset at Mallory Dock,' he said, standing as she drew on her shorts.

She nodded, remembering how they had seen it together, sharing the same pleasure in nature's beauty. And afterwards how they'd gone to the picnic. She darted a swift glance at him. Did he ever think of that picnic? She remembered his kiss. Better leave that memory alone.

'Buy you breakfast?' he asked.

'No, I don't think so. I want to go home and shower off this salt water.'

'I saw a bakery on my way here. How about I get some rolls and croissants and come to your place? I can be there by the time you're finished showering.'

'No. I don't think so.'

He reached out and gently turned her to face him, his hands

light on her shoulders, his touch warm and caressing.

'Hey, Katie, let's be civilized. We'll have one of those divorces where everyone stays friends. How about it? The bakery smelled delicious when I passed.'

She wavered, looked into his eyes, and was uncertain at what she saw. His look was guarded, no hint to what he was feeling. Michael was a master at that. She hesitated, but didn't want to appear afraid to spend time with him. At last, reluctantly, she agreed.

'Okay. But I need at least fifteen minutes.'

She gave him directions to her apartment, watching him as he walked along the beach towards the center of town, wondering if she was doing the right thing. She followed him with her eyes until he was too far away to see. He moved easily, smoothly with just a hint of arrogance and assurance. Like a wolf on the prowl, she thought, unable to move as she watched him.

When he rounded the corner, she turned, and moved slowly towards her apartment. She didn't want to be enemies with him, but was this a wise move?

Katie took a quick shower, hastily towel-dried her hair, and pulled on shorts and a soft yellow cotton shirt, dashing from her bedroom to make sure the rest of her apartment was tidy. It was the first time Michael would see it and she wanted it to look its best. It could not compare with the expensive furnishings of their place in Boston, but that always reminded Katie of a museum. At least her place was warm and inviting.

Satisfied by the time Michael knocked on her door, she looked around once more, wondering how he would like it. It didn't matter; it suited her.

Nervously, she opened the door. If he said anything derogatory about her place, she would slam it shut in his face.

He, however, merely handed her the bag of warm croissants,

stepped in and closed the door. He stood for a moment survey-
ing the apartment, his eyes swiftly assessing the clever ways of
blending different furnishings to create a pleasant setting.

Katie tilted her chin up at him, ready to defend her home if
he said anything disparaging.

With a gleam in his eye, he leaned over and kissed her, one
hand tangling in the still-damp curls, his lips tasting of the salt
air. She was breathless with the intensity of feeling unleashed at
his touch, and her legs grew weak.

He released her, and studied her face for a long moment.

'You can't do that.' Her voice was softer than she had meant
it to be. She cleared her throat.

'Of course I can. We're still married. Besides, I like it.' Satisfied with what he saw on her face, he again looked around the
room, his hand dropping to his side. 'It's nice, comfortable and
restful. Is this what you wanted at our place?'

She turned to the small kitchen. The sun streamed in the
open window—the room was warmer than the rest of the apartment, which probably accounted for her own warm cheeks.

'I wanted to make it more–I don't know, more comfortable,
or welcoming or homey. I always felt it was like a museum.'

She looked shyly at him through her lashes to see if she'd
hurt his feelings. She'd always thought he took great pride in his
house.

'It's very like your aunt's. I thought you'd like it.' His face was
impassive; he gave nothing away.

'I always hated Aunt Margaret's house for the same reason.'
She smiled ruefully. 'It's just me. Everyone else always admired
it. I wanted something–warmer.'

She measured the coffee into the filter, then pulled down
two cups and three plates.

'And how would you change it?'

She glanced up sharply at this. 'Doesn't matter; I'm not going back.'

Michael fell silent, studying the young woman before him. When the coffee was ready, he turned and opened her refrigerator and pulled out butter and jam.

'You still take cream in your coffee?' he asked, balancing the small container with the others.

'Yes.'

Quickly Katie set the table, poured the coffee and sat opposite Michael. He opened the bag and dumped the rolls and croissants on the third plate. Their savory aroma instantly filled the small kitchen.

Katie was confused. Michael wasn't getting any ideas of domesticity, was he? He moved around the kitchen as if it were his. They hadn't often gone into their own kitchen. Frances had always prepared anything they wanted.

'When did the attorneys say the divorce would be final?' Might as well let him know breakfast changed nothing.

'In a few months. They'll send you papers you need to sign.' He reached for a warm croissant.

Katie waited expectantly for Michael to again urge her to change her mind, to stop the proceedings. But he calmly added strawberry jam and bit into it.

She sipped her coffee. Had he really accepted her decision? His suggestion on the beach that they be friends indicated he had. Now, no comments about stopping the divorce. Good. She was relieved.

Or was she? Deep down inside a small twinge of disappointment and sadness touched her.

'Michael, what are you going to do? Here, I mean,' Katie asked.

'Take a much-needed vacation, I guess. We never took a vacation, did we?'

'No, business always came first. I'm surprised they haven't tracked you down here,' she said, striving for lightness.

His look was enigmatic. After a moment he looked away. 'They don't know I'm in Key West,' he said, pouring another cup of coffee.

'Don't know? Why ever not? How will Donovan Construction get on?' She was startled to learn he had, in essence, hidden out. She'd never known him to be out of touch before.

Michael shrugged. 'If it can't get on with the managers I pay a good salary to, then I might as well let it fold. No one's indispensable in business.'

Katie stared at him, unable to believe what she was hearing. She'd never seen Michael like this. Had he changed? Where was the ruthless business-orientated man she knew? It was almost as if he didn't care about business any more. Yet it had been his whole life.

Again she realized how little she knew the man.

'What's the matter? Think I can't take a vacation?' he asked her whimsically.

'I've never known you to do so. Won't you get bored?'

'No, Katie, I won't get bored. I have things to do. One very important thing.' He finished the last of his croissant.

Katie shivered slightly, almost as if it was a warning. Catching sight of the clock, she hastily stuffed the last bite of her roll into her mouth.

'I have to go to work,' she said. She swallowed the last of her coffee. 'Thank you for the croissants; they were delicious.'

A gleam struck Michael's eye as he lifted a lazy smile in her direction. Katie felt the warmth of his smile touch her whole being. She was caught up in his gaze and couldn't break free. Her heart began pounding, and she felt a curious lassitude invade her body.

'Maybe we can do it again one day.' He rose effortlessly and cleared his place, reaching out to take Katie's plate, too. She watched him, puzzled by his thoughtfulness, his attentiveness. What was he up to?

He turned from the sink and leaned over her, one hand on the table, his other on the back of her chair. Katie had to tilt her head back to see him. The blood roared in her ears at his nearness; she could feel awareness rise, conscious of his proximity, the faint lines radiating from his dark eyes, the strong line of his jaw, the smoothness of his skin. She tried to look away. Her fingers longed to touch him, feel the texture of his skin, the supple muscles moving beneath her. Dear God, much more of this would be madness.

'You're sure, are you, Katherine, that you don't want to try again? We could pretend we just met, get to know each other, see if we like what we find.' His voice was low and seductive and sexy.

Katie was drowning in unsuspected longings and desires.

When his lips touched hers, she sighed softly as her whole body clamored for his touch. She'd been wanting him to kiss her. Eagerly she returned his kiss; the brightness behind her closed lids rivaled that of the streaming sunbeams, the warmth of his lips equaled that of the sun, the soft taste of sweet strawberries on his lips tilted her world.

Michael's lips were warm, possessive, plundering the sweet softness of hers, giving pleasure, demanding a response Katie was only too willing to give. Michael's very touch was electric and she was shaken to her soul.

He pulled back, his dark eyes glittering down at her, his gaze centering on her lips. She felt weak, defenseless, bereft. Was that what he wanted? She tried to read the answer in his face.

'I want you, Katherine,' he said urgently.

'No.' She shot back her chair, and pushed against him, shocked at how fast his heart was beating when her hand touched the hard muscles of his chest. Wanting to escape, escape the clamoring of her senses, the overwhelming desire he sparked, she stared up at him with angry, confused eyes.

'No, you don't want me, or if you do it's only because of the challenge to get me, not let something slip through your hands.'

'You're wrong; I want you for you. I've always wanted you. But I can wait. Wherever you are, there I'll be. When you turn around, you'll see me. What we have is too precious to let go.'

He stared boldly down at her, his tone solemn and serious. This was the man she knew. Once he decided on a course, he didn't deviate from it.

'No. I'm not going back to what we had, Michael,' she told him.

'And I told you it needn't be what we had. We can discover each other all over and move on from there.'

'There's nothing to discover. I know you, and know how you operate. My leaving is only a challenge to you, a game.'

'You're my wife and I don't want to let you go.'

'You have no choice, I left.'

'And I want you to come back.'

' Leave me alone,' she cried.

His hand encircled the hand on his chest and he drew it up to his mouth, placing a hot kiss in her palm. Folding her fingers closed, he let her go.

'You going to work now?' His tone was normal; only the glitter of his eyes let Katie know his emotions ran as high as hers.

Katie blinked at the change; she was trembling. She hardly knew what she was doing. Her equilibrium was shattered. She glanced around to get her bearings. How could so much happen in such a short time? Her kitchen looked the same, but was forever changed. She could never eat here again without seeing Michael, reliving his touch, his lips on hers, hearing the words that thundered in her mind.

Taking a deep breath, she tried to get control, seeking calmness and serenity. She'd had years of practice hiding her feelings, acting as appropriate for the situation—proper Bostonian behavior. It stood her in good stead now.

'I have to go.' She grabbed her purse and keys and moved to the front of the apartment, Michael right behind her. She had to escape, had to get free of him. She couldn't think with him so close.

'What time do you get off work? We could go snorkeling,' he said as she opened the door.

'I have plans,' she bit out, afraid to even look at him. She was trembling inside. He was so determined; was she strong enough to hold out against him?

'Maybe tomorrow. I'll check with you then,' he said easily.

She breathed a sigh of relief. Obviously his words had been figurative, said to make a point. He was not going to force himself on her. He couldn't make her want to return. It had taken all her courage to leave. She wouldn't be able to do it again. He had to let her go now.

She took her bike to avoid walking with him to work. She needed to be alone, to recover from breakfast—to recover from Michael's overwhelming presence and the vague yearnings that she dare not give name to.

His words echoed in her mind throughout the day. Katie tried to brush them away. It only worked for a few minutes at a time.

There was really nothing he could do, she reminded herself

constantly. The divorce was progressing. He certainly had never hinted that he'd oppose it. Things would work out—he'd get tired of vacationing and return to Boston.

What if he didn't leave; what if he stayed?

She shook her head. Impossible. Work would demand his attention, or he'd get bored doing nothing in Key West. He couldn't stay—could he?

6

Katie half way expected Michael to be waiting for her when she left work, so she wasn't surprised when she saw him seated by the curb. She didn't speak as she pushed her bike off the resort grounds and onto the street. The afternoon was warm, the streets full of bikini-clad tourists, their skin in various shades of pink and brown.

'I've rented a bike.' He gestured to where one lay propped against some bushes. 'I can accompany you home,' he said.

'What if I'm not going home?' she replied, studying his bike for a moment, then looking at him. He was tenacious, she'd give him that.

'Then I'll go wherever you're going.'

'Leave me alone,' she said firmly.

'You didn't always find my presence bothersome,' he said, trailing his fingers lightly down one bare arm.

Katie jerked back as if she'd been burned.

'Michael, why are you doing this to me?'

'I want you to come home.' His voice was low, his eyes sincere as he gazed down into hers.

'This is my home now.'

She got on the bike and quickly stormed down the street, not looking right nor left until she reached her apartment. Only as she stopped and glanced around did she realize she was alone. That did surprise her.

The phone was ringing when she reached her door. She hurried with the lock and darted across the room when the door finally yielded.

'Katherine?' said the voice at the other end of the phone.

'Aunt Margaret.' Katie was startled to hear her aunt's voice, and felt a little guilty. She hadn't let her aunt know where she was. It had been five and a half months since she'd left and she'd not contacted her once. Not that they were close by any means, but she should have at least let her know where to find her.

'Yes, your Aunt Margaret, the woman who gave you a home when your parents died, who raised you, giving you every advantage money could buy. The same aunt whom you've ignored entirely for the last six months.'

Katie hated her aunt's martyred sarcasm, but it was part and parcel of her. And this time she had cause to be angry.

'I'm sorry I didn't let you know where I was,' Katie said, sitting down on the chair beside the phone.

'You didn't even see fit to tell me you were leaving town. I raised you better than that, Katherine. If life with Michael became intolerable, why not come home?'

Katie thought bleakly of Aunt Margaret's house, furnished in the same opulent manner as Michael's; of her aunt's rigid social behavior, strict attention to duty as she saw it, no matter how unpleasant. Her aunt's sense of duty came first no matter what. It would not have been a sanctuary. Her aunt would have sent her right back to Michael.

'I needed to get away from Boston,' she said.

'Harringtons do not divorce, Katherine. When Michael told me that's what you wanted, I was shocked.'

'I couldn't go on with the way things were. I want more from life than what I had.'

'Good grief, Katherine, Michael lavished things on you;

there were no worries on that front. And you're on all the important committees in Boston.' For her aunt there could be no more.

'Not enough.' Katie spoke more abruptly than she had intended, but a suffocating sensation gripped her throat.

'I can't imagine why not,' her aunt snapped.

'I want to do more than be on committees with a bunch of other women. I want to find out what I like doing, who I am; have friends who like me for me, not because I'm on the fine arts committee or because I'm married to the very successful Michael Donovan. I want a family, children who can run and play and not be so concerned to do everything just right, be utterly correct. I don't want to grow old and regret all I missed.'

There was a long moment of silence then her aunt's voice changed. 'And are you finding that there?'

'I'm having a wonderful time. I have a job. I've learned to snorkel. And I have some really interesting friends who are very different from me, yet we like similar activities and I'm learning lots from them. Actually, I'm really very happy here.'

'You always liked the warmer climates.'

Katie thought back to all the trips her aunt had taken her on. They'd visited all the renowned spots in the world, from the Cote d'Azur to Hong Kong. But one expensive hotel was very much like another, and Katie had been too closely chaperoned to wander the side streets of the places they visited to get a real feel for the country they were in. Lying on the beach had been the closest thing to freedom she'd enjoyed on those trips.

'It's wonderful here, warm and sunny. I can't believe Boston is under snow. They've never even had a frost here on Key West,' she said. She wished she could convince her aunt that this was her future.

'Where are you staying?'

'I have a small apartment.'

'Michael is at the Monarch, I believe.' Aunt Margaret's tone implied that was the only place to stay. Katie suppressed a sigh of frustration. Her aunt wouldn't change. She would always be old ideals, old money, old Boston.

'Katherine, call me if you need anything. You're all I have in the world.'

'I apologize I didn't call you or write you—I just need to be on my own.'

'Not totally on your own. You're a part of my life, my family. If you need anything from me, I will provide it.'

'Thank you, Aunt Margaret.'

Katie hung up the phone, touched by her aunt's last comment. It was the closest she would come to lending tacit approval to her niece's activities. Katie wished they had been closer. But her aunt was not a very warm, nurturing person, and had never sought close ties with her niece. She was quite self-sufficient and content with her own life the way she had structured it. Katie knew she'd been a disruption to Margaret's life when she ended up living with her after her parent's death. She sometimes wondered how life would have been if her parents had lived.

Katie sank down on the sofa, at a loss as to what to do next. If she ventured out, she could run into Michael. Yet if she didn't, she was letting him run her life again, and that was something she refused to do.

Blast Michael. She was making a life without him, was trying to live on her own. How dare he intrude without invitation, entrenching himself in her thoughts, invading her peace and evoking longings she didn't want. Why had he returned to Key West? Just to plague her?

Lying back against the cushions, she closed her eyes, immediately seeing Michael as she'd seen him today, casually attired, his attention on her. He seemed different. Younger without the stress he lived under.

His touch brought reactions she'd hadn't had in years—several years actually. His kisses were exciting, had her yearning for more. His very touch brought responses she couldn't deny. Was it Michael, or her, or the magic of Key West?

Why wouldn't he go away and leave her alone?

Resting her head back on the sofa, she let the warm afternoon air blowing in from the window calm her. There was a hint of sweet fragrance, drifting on the breeze from the frangipani that grew in abundance, so pleasant, so soothing. It was an idyllic spot—if only Michael hadn't come.

What was she going to do?

Determination born of a strong resolve moved her to action. She refused to hide out. She'd do what she damn well pleased and ignore Michael. Or maybe see how far he'd go to infiltrate her new life. Could he stay the course?

Katie freshened up, changed into her swimsuit and a fresh pair of shorts and top, and wheeled out her bike. She rode slowly up Duval Street. She'd see if she could find any of her friends, and maybe go swimming or just grab a snack somewhere and talk.

She saw Rick parked in his cab along the curb, and rode over to him.

'Hi, Katie, what's up?' he called.

'Hi.' She stopped by his window, keeping a wary eye out for oncoming traffic. 'Looking for something to do; have you seen anyone around? I'm looking for a game of volleyball or someone to go swimming with.'

'Saw Jim a while ago, walking towards home. He seems down. Don't know why he'd be home so early in the day unless he's sick. I'm off this shift at four; we might get a volleyball game together then.'

'Okay. I'll find Jim. Look for us when you're off,' Katie told him.

She waved and pushed off, quickly cycling the few blocks to the two story, spread out apartment house where Jim lived. Locking her bike in one of the bike-racks that were spaced randomly along the pavements, she entered the courtyard and headed for his apartment door.

'Hi, Katie, what brings you here?' Jim opened the door, surprised to see her.

She looked at him; he had loosened his tie, shed his suit jacket and looked worn out. 'What's up with you home this early? Are you sick?'

'My big deal fell through; they decided to go to Miami. The principles decided they wanted a bigger bank, not the likes of little Key West. Dammit'

He hit his fist against the wall. 'Come in. Maybe you can cheer me up. I'll never get anywhere in this backwater. I worked damned hard on that deal, too. I really thought it was a shoe-in.'

'Oh, I'm so sorry.' Katie knew how hard he'd worked on that particular piece of business; it was all he'd talked about for the last few weeks. He'd been so proud to be involved on a business venture the magnitude of this one. She sat on the edge of one of his chairs as Jim paced the small living room.

'Same old story. Everyone wants bigger and better. Our bank just won't make it. I've got to get off this island. I'll go crazy if I don't.' He looked over at her, narrowing his gaze.

'What about your friend Michael? I heard he was back. He must do okay where he works to afford to stay at the Monarch. Could he put in a word for me somewhere? Does he know any bankers? Networking's the key.'

Katie leaned back in her chair, her thoughts spinning. Of course Michael used big banks, and the deals he made put Jim's efforts in the shade. Her husband was used to dealing in tens of millions of dollars, had letters of credit for several of the largest banks in Boston and New York.

Not that she could ask for his help. She was trying to separate herself from the man, not put herself in his debt. She dare not ask a favor at this point.

She shook her head slowly. 'I don't think so.'

'Oh, please, Katie, help me out,' Jim urged. 'I'm dying down here. I've got to get into something better and without some kind of connection I don't have a chance. Can't you at least ask?' His face reflected his desperation, his tone beseeching.

Katie hesitated. The last thing she wanted was to be in Michael's debt. Yet she didn't want to explain the situation to Jim—it would be too long and involved. Even then, Jim might not understand. All he wanted was help from any source.

She knew if Jim had the right connections, he'd go far. He was driven, conscientious and hardworking. To have friends, she needed to be friends. And it wouldn't take much for Michael to put a good work in at a couple of places.

'I guess I could ask him,' she said slowly.

She'd rather do almost anything than ask a favor, but Jim put her on the spot. She glanced at him again. His face lost some of the anger and frustration that had been there moments before. He seemed almost excited again.

'Great, thanks, Katie. If he knows anyone it would be a help. Will you ask him today?'

'The next time I see him,' she stalled. Maybe she wouldn't see him for a few days. Maybe Jim would feel better abut things later and it wouldn't be so important to him.

'Want to go to the beach? Rick's looking for others for a game.' Katie changed the subject.

'Yeah, might as well. I'll get on my suit.'

He talked to her through the open door as he changed, telling her how his deal had fallen through; how the investors at the last moment revealed they'd been unsure about his bank and had already been negotiating with a larger bank.

'It's the last straw, Katie. I just can't continue to live down here. It's driving me crazy,' he said.

She'd known he was unhappy and discontent with the slower pace of life in Key West. Ever since she'd met him, he'd been talking of doing big things just to get the recognition he felt he needed to move to a bigger city, a bigger job and a chance at life in the fast lane.

Michael could definitely help him, if he would. She didn't know how to ask, however. She tried to picture various scenarios for asking. Should she seek him out or wait until they happened to be together? Should she hint around, hoping he'd rise to the bait, or just flatly ask for the favor?

She sighed; she hated doing it, however she approached it. Would he give her a straight yes or no? Or cross-examine her the way he did the businessmen he dealt with on important issues? Flat out refuse unless she returned to Boston.

'Ready.' Jim had changed to shorts, a cotton shirt left open covered his shoulders and arms, and he wore sandals on his feet.

He gave her a hug when she stood.

'You're great to help me out, Katie. I really appreciate it.'

'No problem.' At least she hoped it wouldn't be a problem.

A horn tooted as they stepped out onto the sidewalk and she turned around, Jim's arm companionably across her shoulder. Rick's cab drew to the curb and he grinned at them.

'Want a ride? Free to friends as of now. I'm almost finished for today. Climb in.'

Debbie and Marlise were in the front with Rick. When Jim opened the back door, Katie started to climb in, startled to find

Michael's dark eyes glittering across at her. She paused, then slid into the back seat, scooting across to the middle to give Jim room. She had to move right up to Michael; the heat of his body felt from shoulder to knee. She glanced at him from the corner of her eye, looked quickly away when she saw his penetrating look. He seemed angry.

Now what had she done? Or was he just mad because she'd escaped his surveillance for a few hours?

'Hello, Michael,' she said. To remain silent would cause comment from the others.

'Katie. Jim.' His voice was neutral, but the glitter in his eyes showed strong emotion.

Katie shivered despite the heat and she looked out of Jim's window. She felt oddly vulnerable, sad almost. She didn't want Michael mad at her. He'd said they should keep their separation friendly; could they do that?

'Michael's up for volleyball, too,' Rick said as he pulled away from the curb. 'Some of the others will meet us there. If we don't have enough, we'll pick up some players from people on the beach.'

Jim nudged her; when she looked up at him he nodded towards Michael. Katie gave a quick jerk of her head to indicate she knew what he meant, but she had to ask in her own time. And that time was certainly not now in a car full of people. She wanted to be alone with Michael when she requested his help. There was no telling what he would say and she didn't want to be in front of others when he replied.

The day was warm, but the heat Katie felt was not due entirely to the weather. The car was close, even with all the windows open, and the side of her body felt scorched by Michael's touch. She swallowed hard, trying to ignore him, trying to listen to the light-hearted banter in the front seat. But every sense was attuned to Michael.

His legs were slightly spread, his thigh brushing against hers, moving imperceptibly against her soft skin. She tried to move her legs, but the confined space of the car didn't allow much leeway. She threw him a warning look, but he was staring straight ahead, a slight smile on his lips.

When Rick turned, Michael slid slowly into Katie, his weight resting against her for a minute. She caught her breath, his face only inches from her own.

'Sorry,' he murmured, moving to the corner, yet letting his arm continue to touch hers, his leg never leaving hers.

Katie could scarcely breathe. Nerve-endings tingled as her awareness of the body beside her grew. His hands were mere inches from her own tanned legs; he had only to move a fraction and he could caress her.

She drew in a sharp breath. If this didn't stop, she'd explode. Where were they? How much further to the beach?

They paid the fee to enter the Fort Zachary Taylor Park—the ruins of the old fort from the Civil War. The beach was one of the favorites around town and they used it often.

At least she could get out of the car, away from such close proximity to Michael. He hadn't said a word to her since they'd set off. She should be so lucky to have that continue.

Jim nudged her again, wagging his eyebrows, urging her to talk with Michael.

She sighed, about to scream with exasperation. She only wanted to get away from Michael, from the suffocation she felt near him, and Jim continued to pressure her. She would do it, but at the time of her choosing.

'Okay, you guys set up while I turn the cab in. I'll be back as soon as I can get here,' Rick said as he dropped them near the beach. Debbie and Michael hauled the volleyball net and poles from the trunk, Katie grabbed the bag that contained the ball and towels, standing as far from Michael as she could. If she took a few deep breaths her heart rate should settle down—she hoped.

Following the others to the beach, she was still trying to decide how and when to ask Michael. Jim dropped back.

'You're going to ask him, aren't you?' he said.

'Yes, give me a little time; I want to get a positive answer, not just blurt out the question. I said I'd do it, and I will.' She was abrupt, but her nerves were already stretched tight and she didn't need more pressure from Jim.

'Okay. It's just so important to me.'

Katie tried to remember that as she smiled at her friend. 'I know it is. I don't know if he can give any help, but I'll ask when I think the time is right.'

Katie watched as the men set up the net, standing a bit apart from Debbie and Marlise, her eyes following Michael as he worked. Planting the pole and stringing the nets was short work for a man of his stature. He looked as much at home at the beach as he did in his office.

What would be the best way to ask him? The question replayed itself in her mind like a broken record. Would he refuse outright? Or make some sort of demand in return? She wished Jim had never brought up the subject. Why couldn't he ask himself? He was the one who wanted the favor, after all.

When Michael finished setting up the net, he turned, his eyes clashing with Katie's. Holding her gaze, he walked over to her until he stood so close that she had to tilt her head back to see him.

'What's with you and Jim?' he asked, his voice cold.

She blinked at him, surprised at the question.

'He's one of my friends here. You met him before.'

'How close a friend? You were coming from his apartment with his arm around you when we drove up.'

'Oh, that.' She stalled for time. She didn't want to blurt out her request; she wanted time to work up to it gradually. 'I was waiting for him to change. And told him I'd do something for him, and he was glad, that's all. I didn't expect to see you here.'

He glanced around, looking back directly at her. 'I told you I'd be around,' he reminded her softly.

He shrugged out of his shirt; his shorts rode low on his hips, his skin still not darkly tanned, but the pink had changed to brown. Katie looked at him, dragged her eyes away and stared at the net. She couldn't think with him so near. Every nerve tingled this close to the man.

'I don't want to get burned.' He handed her a bottle of sunscreen and turned his back to her.

She stared at him, her heart starting a slow, heavy pounding. Pouring some of the lotion on her hand, she tentatively reached out and spread it over his shoulders.

His skin was warm from the sun, the muscles firm and supple beneath her touch. Her fingers smoothed the lotion, reveling in the touch of his skin, the leashed strength she felt. She poured more lotion, dropped the bottle to the sand and used both hands to smooth the sunscreen over his broad back. Her hands moved over his shoulders, down to his tapering waist and to the top of his low-riding shorts; up again, over the muscles beside his backbone, along the powerful ones of his shoulders, down again. She stopped thinking, only felt the pleasure of his skin, the delight her hands enjoyed against him.

Katie's emotions were in turmoil. Her hands enjoyed touching this man, drawing the heat from his body and the sun into her own, moving over the fine sculpture of his back, touching him, helping him. Yet she dared not let him know it.

Abruptly, Michael turned to face her, stopping and picking up the bottle. He took her hand and poured more lotion into it.

'Do my chest,' he ordered.

She rubbed her two hands together to distribute the lotion, then slowly reached out to spread it on his skin. She knew instantly that it had been a mistake. The intimacy of facing him and spreading lotion on his chest was ten times that of spreading it on his back. She kept her eyes firmly on the task at hand, refusing to look up to meet his gaze, though she could feel his eyes burning down at her. Concentrating on breathing, hoping her erratic heartbeat wasn't clearly visible to him, she reached out.

She smoothed the lotion over his shoulders, then down again to tangle her fingers in the crisp dark hair covering his chest. When her fingers brushed his nipples, Michael drew in a sharp breath. Startled, Katie's eyes flew up to lock with his. She snatched her hands away as if they were on fire.

His hands covered hers and drew them back to his chest, while his eyes stared down into hers. Slowly she moved her hands against him, up and down, pulling slightly against the hair on his chest, avoiding his nipples, trying to break the hold he had on her. She felt drawn into a swirling vortex from which she didn't think she could escape.

Her hands had a life of their own, moving as they willed over his hot skin, touching him, caressing him, conscious that her touch was affecting Michael as much as it was her. Her body longed for his touch, longed for him to caress her–as she was caressing him. Her breathing became restricted and she opened her lips for more breath, her eyes looking at Michael's mouth. Would he kiss her? Her lips tingled in anticipation, in longing.

'Sweet hell, Katherine, that's what you're putting me through.' His voice was low, soft, carrying only to her ears. 'If there weren't dozens of people around I'd make love to you right here and now.' His hand covered hers, stopping their wanderings. His fingers laced through hers and he held their hands against his skin, his eyes meeting hers again, the longing and desire clearly evident.

Katie drew a deep, shaky breath, reason starting to penetrate. Slowly she shook her head, wanting to deny her feelings, wanting to deny him. But no sound came to her lips.

'Hey, you two, are you going to play volleyball or what?' Rick's amused voice carried over the pounding in Katie's ears. Had he returned already? How long has she and Michael been there?

She snatched her hands back and looked over toward the net. There were several people set up to play. Obvious gaps showed where she and Michael should join in.

With a quick, uncertain peek at Michael, she moved to join Jim and Debbie's side near the net. Michael joined the opposing team. Both he and Jim played the game to win. Several times during the game Katie was struck with the similarity between the two of them. Jim was young yet, but determined and competitive. Most of them were playing for the fun of the contest, but not Jim and Michael. Their will to win dominated their game. Jim would easily fit in to Michael's world. She only had to give him the assistance, ask the favor of Michael, and get him to agree.

Several times during the fast-paced game she hit a ball over only to have it slammed back to their side, the glint in Michael's eyes revealing savage triumph as his team pulled ahead. She tried harder, but each time she'd hit a ball over he'd return it, rarely giving his teammates a chance against her moves.

Michael played the game ruthlessly, all out to win. Katie fought back, but grew more and more frustrated as it became apparent to her what he was doing. She wanted to stop him, defeat him, prove to herself that she could put some sort of dent in the man—even if only in a game. But none of the others on her team played as ruthlessly, as determinedly, not even Jim.

Slowly, steadily, Michael's team drew ahead. His serves were powerful, impossible to return. When he was near the net, his spikes were constant. The pleasure in the game was lost as Katie only tried to fight against him.

Again and again their eyes clashed, the unspoken duel clear to both. As the game played out, Katie became angrier, while Michael became mocking, as her attempts to best him proved inadequate.

At last it was over. His eyes glittered at her in triumph. The others laughed and criticized the game, regrouping to play again and mix the teams. But Katie had enough. Calling farewell to her friends, she put on her sandals and hurried for Duval Street, trying to get as far from Michael as she could. She'd get her bike and go home; lock her door and remove the phone from the hook.

She reckoned without him following her. She had not reached the gate to the park before he caught up with her.

'Katherine.'

She stopped, and slowly turned around, frowning when she saw how close he was.

'What?' She only wanted to escape.

'Where are you going? We're playing another game.' He stopped within inches of her, within easy touching distance.

'I don't want to play games with you any more. You're ruthless.' She took a step back.

'I play to win.' His voice was quiet, threatening.

'Yes, and I play volleyball for fun. It wasn't fun today.'

'I enjoyed it.'

He had put back on his shirt, but left it unbuttoned. The expanse of brown chest that showed was powerful, masculine, drawing her eyes. She tried to avoid him, but her eyes were drawn back again and again. Only an hour or so ago she had spread lotion on the warm skin now partially covered by his shirt. Her fingers remembered. She longed to reach out and trail her fingers down that broad expanse, stop fighting and—

'Go play with the others. I don't want to,' she told him.

'What do you want to do?' he asked softly.

'I want to go home. I want you to leave me alone.'

'I don't think you know what you want, Katherine. But I can wait.'

She looked away, then back at him, standing so strong in the afternoon sun. Self-assured, confident, determined.

It was the wrong time, she knew it, but she couldn't help it. It was now or never as far as she was concerned. With any luck she wouldn't see him again for a few days. Prolonged dithering wasn't going to make it any easier.

'I do want a favor,' she said, looking away again, across the sand to the turquoise and blue of the sea.

'What?' Gone was the soft tone. His voice became wary.

She chanced a glance at his face. It had gone remote and closed. Not the most auspicious time to ask. She should wait, but she plunged ahead.

'Jim wants an introduction to a bigger banking firm than where he works now. I thought you could give him an in with one of those banks you deal with.' She said it quickly, bluntly, without any explanation.

His eyes narrowed as he stared down at her as if assessing the question, seeking motives, weighing the possible outcomes.

'Why?' he asked.

'He doesn't like it here. He's the only native I know, and wants desperately to get off Key West. I thought you could help him.'

'Why should I?'

Her mind went blank. She couldn't think of a single reason why he should—at least not the way he thought.

'To help out. It wouldn't cost you anything,' she said finally.

Michael was silent so long that Katie thought he was ignoring her request. She almost spoke again when he replied, 'It will cost you.'

She looked surprised. 'Cost me? What?'

He paused a moment, then leaned forward, his face almost touching hers. 'Sleep with me again.'

7

Katie's eyes widened as she realized what he'd said. Color stained her cheeks. How dare he proposition her because of her request.

'You're crazy.'

'Actually, I'm a businessman. I have something you want, you have something I want. We make a deal. Think on it. I told you I want you. If you wish for me to do something for your friend, you decide how badly you want it. That's the deal.'

'I think you're an arrogant, ruthless bastard,' she spit out.

'Maybe, but I want you most damnably.'

'Never.'

'Careful, Katherine, never is a very long time. You don't know what the future holds.'

'I know it doesn't hold me sleeping with you again.'

'You never know.' His voice was soft, no anger showed. 'I think it would be quite different from what we've shared in the past. You're a different woman from the sheltered young woman I married. Here you're different from a proper Bostonian wife. I think making love to you now would be hot and wild and passionate. You'd give more than you ever have before, and you'd get more than you ever have before. Think of it, Katherine— one night of wild, hot abandoned passion between us. We started out good. Somewhere along the way we lost our way. But once—for old time's sake.'

Her heart leapt at his words, pounding, hot blood rushing through her veins. They'd been so in love when they married. Those first few months had been heavenly.

'I knew I shouldn't have asked. I'll tell Jim to forget it.' She tried to drag her eyes from his, but couldn't do it.

'As long as you tell him that it's in your power to get him his introduction, and that you refuse,' he taunted.

'I'd never tell him such a thing. Even if I ever did he wouldn't want me to lower myself to your request.'

'Oh, for God's sake, Katherine. We're married. It's not lowering yourself to anything.'

'No.' She whirled and ran the last few yards to the gate. Then, slowing to a fast walk, she headed for home. She'd get her bike tomorrow. She only wanted the sanctuary of her apartment, the security of her own place, where Michael couldn't penetrate, couldn't throw her life in turmoil.

She was humiliated, angered and cheapened by Michael's suggestion. How dared he? She was not some slut to offer her body in exchange for favors. Especially not when she was trying to end their relationship.

Her anger had not abated by the time she reached her apartment. She slammed the door furiously behind her, momentarily ashamed of the racket she caused. There was no need to upset all her neighbors. But her concern was fleeting. Unable to contain her anger, she paced the small room, her fists clenched furiously.

How dared he suggest such a thing? She paused, her mind flooded with unbidden pictures of the two of them in bed, the kisses hot and tumultuous, reminiscent of his kisses on the beach. Her hands yearned to touch his skin, as she had this afternoon, her body craved his touch. Would their lovemaking be fiery, stormy, tempestuous in the sultry tropical night?

His idea was an insult, preposterous, outrageous.

Yet, despite her best intentions, she thought of little else during the long evening. Even as she went to bed, the idea of it churned in her head. Deep within her was the small desire to see what it would be like. She was different now. The few times he'd kissed her on the island, she'd flared with passion and desire.

Their early months together had been rapturous, exciting, fulfilling. It was only after work became all-encompassing that their sex life had tapered off, come to a halt. She had always thought of making love as enjoyable. Yet the encounters with Michael on Key West proved that wrong. The passionate, raw, almost primitive, spectacular feelings made enjoyable too tepid a word to describe them.

Katie didn't venture out until it was time to go to work the next morning. She chose a route different from her normal one and saw no one she knew before she reached the hotel.

When she left work in the afternoon, she expected Michael to be by the employees' entrance. He was not. For a moment, she felt a twinge of disappointment. Shaking her head at her own inconsistency, she strolled home, glad he was not around. Maybe he finally listened to her.

When she turned into her street, however, she saw him. He was sitting on the front steps of her building, reading a newspaper. As she drew nearer, she could see it was the Wall Street Journal.

'Can't keep away from it, can you?' Her tone was carefully neutral. She refused to let the bitterness of her feelings spill out when sight of the paper had her spinning back to their life in Boston.

He deliberately folded the newspaper and tossed it aside. Standing, he towered over her, his eyes scanning her figure from head to toe.

'Just reading; it's you I can't keep away from.' His voice was low, sexy, provocative.

Despite herself, Katie felt a spurt of joy surge through her at his words. A smile tugged at her lips. Then his suggestion popped into mind, and instantly she was on the defensive.

'Go on, Michael. We've been over and over this. Nothing's changed. Just go away, let the divorce proceed and let's get on with our lives.'

'I told you I'd be around. Why not just give up now?'

She pushed past him and mounted the stairs to the short hallway.

'Look over your shoulder and I'll be there,' he'd said.

Involuntarily, Katie looked over her shoulder and saw Michael only inches away from her. He'd entered the hallway before the door had closed. He smiled sardonically into her startled face.

'So now you're stalking me?''

She'd like to wipe that knowing, mocking smile from his face—make him understand she was through with him. She raised her hand to push him away. He caught her wrist and pulled her into his arms, giving her a quick kiss.

'Give it up, sweetheart, you don't have a chance! Do you really think I'm stalking you?'

'I do. Go away, Michael. What we had is over. I want my freedom.'

His eyes gazed into hers for a long time. 'Then we'll see.' He lowered his head, his lips capturing hers.

Katie wanted to resist. Maybe if she stood still, let the feelings wash through while she gave nothing back, he'd leave her alone. But it was hard to restrain herself—she longed to kiss him in return, hold his body closer to her, feel the pounding in her veins go on and on, feel the heat he engendered consume her, the delight continue forever.

Michael pulled back, resting his forehead on hers, his eyes dark and mysterious. Bravely she faced him, keeping her face free from all expression. He sighed and stood away from her.

'See you around.' He turned and let himself out of the front door. As soon as the door shut, Katie sank in a heap against the wall. The hardest thing she'd ever done was not returning his kiss.

Katie didn't see Michael for the next couple of days, but he was never far from her thoughts. She watched for him on her way to and from work, at the beach in the mornings. But never saw him. She didn't want to ask Debbie about him, for fear of giving rise to speculation. But she listened intently to the different maids' conversations to pick up any mention of him.

Marlise gave the first clue as to why Katie hadn't seen him around when she and Debbie met her for lunch three days after the volleyball game. They ordered hamburgers and Cokes and sat at one of the outside tables. The colorful umbrella shaded them from the sun's hot rays.

Katie donned sunglasses to hide the dark circles beneath her eyes. She didn't need her friends questioning her about that.

'Haven't seen Michael around much—guess we won't any more,' Marlise said as she spread a liberal amount of ketchup on her french fries.

'Why's that?' Debbie asked, scraping the onion from her burger.

'Got competition now and more in his league.' Marlise looked like the cat that swallowed the canary. She loved to give out gossip.

'Meaning?' Katie asked casually, taking a sip of her Coke.

'Meaning, we now have a young single woman on the make and she's after our Michael. She and her father are down from New York. Only her father's always out on some deep-sea fishing yacht, so Miss Elizabeth Bowman is at loose ends. Or she was until she latched on to Michael.'

'Michael can take care of himself. No one latches on if he doesn't want them to,' Katie murmured.

'True, but who said he didn't want her to? He took her to dinner last night, all duded up in fancy clothes. They went to one of the restaurants in the hotel and I saw them. He was most attentive.'

Katie didn't respond; she felt sick. She picked up her hamburger, wondering if she could possibly eat it. Taking a small bite, she chewed it slowly, forcing it down. She took a sip of Coke.

What was the matter with her? She'd had wanted to end their marriage. This was perfect. If Michael found another woman, he'd be glad to release her. There would be no more problems.

Why wasn't she happier?

As the conversation ebbed and flowed around her, the soft sea breeze caressed her skin. The sun shone from the cloudless blue sky, yet Katie felt as if she were in a cold cave. She didn't remember eating her hamburger, but when she looked it was almost gone. Her drink didn't quench her thirst, but gave her something to do with her hands, and an excuse for not talking.

She wanted to be alone. She tried to follow the conversation between Marlise and Debbie, but couldn't concentrate. Idly she watched people passing, the happy faces of the visitors, the contented ones of the natives. It was a typical afternoon in Key West.

Katie gathered her rubbish and rose. 'I'm off- have some

errands to attend to.' She plastered a smile on her face. Appearance was everything; that she had learned years ago at her aunt's knee.

Once free from observation by her friends, she could relax, but until then she'd keep the silly grin on her face.

She walked down Duval Street, a strange ache in her breast. 'He was most attentive.' Marlise's words echoed and re-echoed in her head. Katie knew how attentive he could be. Knew how charming and compelling he was when he set out to be.

As if the very thought of Michael conjured him up, she saw him before her on the pavement. Beside him was a lovely young woman dressed in an obviously expensive shorts and shirt set. Her dark hair was carefully arranged, her nails long and polished, her complexion clear and tanned.

Katie stopped, flustered. Should she cross the street, pretend she hadn't seen them? Or duck into the nearby T-shirt store? Or—

The decision was taken from her. Michael caught her eye and held it as he drew near and stopped his companion.

'Hello, Katie. Elizabeth, I'd like to introduce you to Katie...Harrington. Katie, Elizabeth Bowman. Elizabeth's staying at the Monarch, too.'

'How do you do?' Katie said, her eyes on Michael, though with dark glasses neither would notice. Beside the elegantly turned-out woman, she felt hot and sticky and unkempt.

'How do you do? Are you staying at the Monarch as well?' There was just a trace of a New York accent.

'No, I work there.' Katie darted another glance at Michael, but his expression gave nothing away. His eyes were hooded as he watched the two women.

'Oh?' Elizabeth looked perplexed.

'Uh, huh, I'm a maid.' Katie smiled as she said it. She recognized Elizabeth for what she was: a snob of the first order. Not for her socializing with the hired help.

Michael's lips twitched slightly and he looked away. Had Katie glimpsed amusement in his eyes?

'I'm sure we'll run into each other often,' Katie continued, giving in to the impish feeling that developed from the pretentious Miss Bowman. 'Key West is such a small, cozy place. Nice to see you again, Michael.'

Katie felt great. Her voice had sounded sincere; none of the turmoil she felt had showed. Michael would never know how much this had cost her. He'd thought to catch her off guard and she'd proved she could hold her own with him.

Elizabeth had manners, if nothing else, and she nodded and smiled politely at Katie. As they walked on, however, Katie could hear her reproach Michael.

'Really, did you have to introduce the maid? Surely the hotel doesn't expect the guests to fraternize with the help.'

Katie couldn't hear Michael's reply. He, of course, had done it deliberately to make sure she knew he was with someone else. Well, that was fine. She was glad for him. Now maybe he'd leave her alone.

Not that he had forced himself on her. She had to be honest. Each encounter at Key West had been partially her own doing. Funny, she didn't think back to their lives in Boston. It was as if they were two different people. The only Michael she thought of now was the one she knew in Key West. And he didn't resemble her husband of the last several years.

Had he changed, or had she? Had she lived in a dream world in Boston, moving through the motions, oblivious to everything that went on around her? Had the Michael of Key West been there all along and she too blind to see? More importantly, if he had been there, had she made a mistake in wanting to end their marriage?

Every time she came into contact with him, she was aware of him physically, of the strong magnetic attraction of the man. She thought back to the conversations they'd had since he arrived in Key West. When he talked to Rick or Jim, his contributions were interesting and insightful. He never condescended when talking to either, though in business both were vastly inexperienced in comparison.

Their private conversations had centered on themselves. No words of love, only of separation and endings. Yet she'd enjoyed breakfast—until his threat; enjoyed their dinner at the Only One. Flushing with the truth, Katie realized she liked his kisses; the desire to repeat them was almost overwhelming, and her lips actually ached in longing.

Sadly, Katie wondered if he had found someone else to take her place, to provide him with a hostess for his functions, someone who would like his house, enjoy the social standing of being Mrs. Michael Donovan? Someone who would want the hot, wild, passionate nights he spoke of?

She fervently hoped it wasn't Elizabeth Bowman. She stopped suddenly, the person behind her bumping into her.

'Sorry.' She moved to the edge of the pavement, stunned with her discovery. She was jealous of Elizabeth! She didn't even know the woman, and she was jealous of her, of her spending time with Michael. Of maybe attracting Michael. Was Katie so small that she didn't want him to find happiness without her? She didn't want to stay married, but that didn't mean that Michael wasn't to marry again.

She'd never thought that far. She'd always pictured him working, devoting endless days and nights to the machinations of big business. But he had lost no time in finding another woman, one, moreover, who would be perfectly suited to his position. One who would probably delight in helping him for business. Be the perfect hostess for social events.

It was impossible. But it was there, nevertheless—she was jealous of a woman she'd just met. Katie resumed walking, considering this strange turn of events. She'd never been jealous of anything in her life. Of course, it was one thing to imagine Michael in Boston at his endless dinners and meetings, quite another to find he was a personable, sexy man, now dancing attendance on another woman. A pretty woman at that.

She had no right to feel as she did. Though feelings quite often didn't do as they should. She wished he was still pursuing her. No, she didn't, did she?

She rather thought she did.

How foolish. One minute wanting a divorce, starting over, doing things just as she wanted, the next, wondering if she had made a mistake.

She let herself into her apartment and went to the kitchen to make a large glass of iced tea. She wouldn't think about it any more. She had made her choice and would stick to it.

She ignored the small ache in her heart.

Jim called that evening. 'Did you talk to Michael?' was his first question.

'Yes... I mean no, not about what you want.' She couldn't tell him Michael's condition for the favor.

'You said you would,' he accused.

'I will, I will, Jim. But it's a big favor and I have to find the right time to ask him.'

'From what I hear from Marlise, you may never get the chance. He's all gaga over some rich woman from New York. Maybe her father could help, too. What do you think?'

Good grief, would he want her to ask Elizabeth next?

'No, let me ask one at a time. I'll try to talk to Michael in the next few days. How are things going at work now?' Maybe it would be better and she could soften the blow of not getting the recommendation.

'It's miserable! I've got to get out. Katie, why don't you throw a party? You could get Michael to come to that, ask him there.'

'I'll find a way, Jim.'

Katie was exasperated. It wasn't as easy as Jim seemed to think. Why did he keep badgering her about it? Should she just tell him Michael had said no? But what if he asked him himself? And found out Michael had said yes, with a caveat? Surely Jim wouldn't want her to sleep with Michael just to get another job. Or would he care? Especially if Michael told him she was his wife!

She was irritated when she hung up. First Elizabeth, now Jim. Why couldn't she be left alone? Her days had used to be so carefree. Once Michael had come, though, it had all changed.

Katie was surprised the next morning to find Michael at the beach when she went for her swim. She smiled involuntarily, then remembered to be on her guard. He had obviously been running and had stopped to wait for her. She watched him warily as she approached the water's edge.

'Good morning,' he said politely, his eyes skimming down the length of her, then coming back to rest on her lips, which Katie licked involuntarily, wishing he'd kiss her again.

'Good morning.' She shed her cover-up and waded into the water. Michael joined her, moving a little ahead to dive into the silky warmth, resurfacing a few feet in front of her.

'This is great—so peaceful early in the morning.'

'Yes.' She dived beneath the swells and gave herself up to the enjoyment of her early morning swim. When she came up for breath, he was near, but not too near. Content to swim beside her, he made no effort at conversation. Katie relaxed and began to enjoy herself.

It was companionable with him there—she was lonely sometimes. It was fun to swim with someone.

'I'm going snorkeling off the coral reef later today; want to go?' he asked.

Katie looked over at him, wondering if there was any ulterior motive. 'I love to snorkel,' she said slowly. 'When are you going?'

'About one; can you get off work?'

'I'd have to see. If I can, I'd like to go. Any conditions?' She faced him, thinking she might as well get it out in the open if there were.

He smiled the lazy smile she saw often here in Key West, and her heart turned somersaults in her breast at the sight. His teeth were white against his tanned face, his eyes dancing in amusement.

'Not today, Katie.'

She thought he was laughing at her, but she suddenly didn't care. She loved snorkeling and didn't get to go to the reef very often. If there were no conditions, she'd grab the chance—if she could get off work early. Maybe Debbie would cover for her and she could swap out with her later in the week.

As they swam back to shore, Katie expected Michael to suggest breakfast together again. But he didn't. She watched him as he dried off, his body brown from the sun, trim and sexy. His shorts clung to his skin—they would dry as he ran, but now revealed his masculinity with shocking clarity. She felt warmth invade her limbs. Looking up to his face, she was startled to find him watching her.

Her hands grew clumsy as he took her towel from her unresisting fingers. Slowly he dried her shoulders, moving down to dry each arm, treating her as if she had no will of her own. Docilely she stood before him, delighting in his touch, in the intimate concept. Taking a ragged breath, Michael wrapped the towel tightly around her body, tucking the ends at the top. The back of his fingers brushed the soft swell of her breasts. Katie gasped, closing her eyes briefly.

When she opened them, he was several feet away, heading for the hotel.

'Meet me at the front desk about one,' was all he said, then he began running again, back towards the hotel.

She watched him go, disappointment warring with relief that he didn't want breakfast with her. Was he eating with Elizabeth? The thought came unbidden. She frowned, hoping that was not the case.

Promptly at one o'clock Katie appeared at the front desk, wearing her swimsuit beneath her shorts, her towel and snorkeling gear in a large canvas tote. She scanned the lobby, looking for Michael. Her heart stopped when she saw him. Happiness swelled within her and a smile touched her lips as he headed her way. His own lazy smile was in evidence as his eyes indolently scanned her from her head to her feet.

'Hope we're not late.' A voice spoke behind Katie—one she instantly recognized. Her heart dropped as she turned to see Elizabeth Bowman approach with a tall, distinguished older man at her side. Elizabeth recognized Katie at the same moment and her expression was one of polite disbelief.

'Everyone's prompt,' Michael said. 'Jack, I'd like to introduce you to Katie. Katie, Jack Bowman, Elizabeth's father. You remember Elizabeth, too, don't you?'

Katie smiled politely at both of them, turning to glare at Michael. Was this his idea of a joke?

Elizabeth obviously didn't find it funny either. 'Really, Michael, I didn't realize we were including... others in our outing.'

'Plenty of room for all—eh, young lady?' Jack Bowman tried to fill the awkward tension. Katie smiled at him and nodded, wishing now she'd questioned Michael further. No conditions, he had said, but he'd made no mention that there would be others either. How civilized was she supposed to be with Michael's— Michael's what?

'The Reef Excursions boat is at Mallory Dock. It leaves at one-thirty. All snorkel equipment on board.' Michael took Elizabeth's arm and gently turned her towards the door. Jack fell into step beside Katie, but she hardly noticed; she was too intent on the couple before her.

Her gaze glued to Michael and Elizabeth as they walked to the dock, she could hardly think, only feel embarrassment and mortification . Was Elizabeth his girlfriend? Was she, Katie, just to stand by while he started dating others? Was he rubbing her nose in his newfound dating freedom?

She caught herself suddenly. Why should she care? She wanted the divorce. She didn't want to be married to Michael, so why shouldn't he find someone else?

But not Elizabeth, she thought fiercely, jealous again at the attention Michael paid her. Not Elizabeth!

A large, sleek white boat was moored at the dock at the foot of Duval Street. Several people were already on board and Katie nimbly stepped across the wide gangplank. She tried to keep her eyes from Michael and Elizabeth, but couldn't help noticing how often the woman needed help—help that Michael was all to ready to provide.

'You a native down here?' Jack asked as he sat beside Katie on the side bench at the back of the boat.

'No, I've only been here a few months,' she replied.

'Wonderful place, Key West; I come here each year to try my hand with deep-sea fishing. Went sail fishing yesterday. Last few days, actually. Caught a small one. Not one I want mounted— but we've another week yet. Maybe I'll get the big one.'

'What will you do with it?' she asked, more to be polite than from interest. Her attention was focused on Elizabeth and Michael, standing near the rear, heads bent close in conversation. She refused to let the sight of them dim her enjoyment of snorkeling. She would have a good time.

'Mount it then display it in my office. I have a couple at home but Elizabeth really doesn't like them.'

'And your wife—what does she think?'

'Don't have one, divorced years ago. Elizabeth's all I have now.' He beamed proudly over at his daughter.

Conversation lagged when the big boat started up. Katie turned so that she could watch towards the front as they headed for the Atlantic and the coral reef. The wind blew through her curls, cooling, refreshing. She loved the sparkling water, the clear blues and aquas and greens. Looking down, she could see the bottom, dozens of feet beneath the surface.

The trip took about forty-five minutes. The captain tied up at one of the approved anchor buoys, designed to minimize damage to the fragile coral reef. The people on board began to don their equipment. There were scuba divers as well as those snorkeling.. Katie would try scuba some day, but for now she was content to snorkel, happy to be here at all. Why had Michael included her? She turned to glance at him. It probably hadn't been from the goodness of his heart. He didn't have one. Was it to show off his new girl before his soon-to- be ex-wife?

As she moved towards the rear of the boat, and the platform that stretched out at water level there, she saw Elizabeth hand Michael her sunscreen. Unable to help herself, Katie watched as Michael applied the lotion to Elizabeth's shoulders, arms and back. Was it her imagination, or did he linger over the task?

She remembered putting the sunscreen on Michael at the beach, and her hands tingled, longing to touch him again; longing to feel his warm skin beneath her fingers, to draw her hands across his strong muscles, feel the movement beneath her. Her whole body warmed at the memory.

She yanked on her mask and adjusted her snorkel. For a moment she almost asked him to spread some lotion on her back. But how foolish that would be. She'd do better to keep her distance from him.

Was he having Elizabeth return the favor? Katie glanced over her shoulder once more, just to see.

Michael's glance caught hers, held it for a long moment, then he dropped his eyes back to the task at hand, his lips lifting in a slight smile.

Flushing with embarrassment at being caught, Katie vowed she would not look their way again. When it was her turn on the platform, she sat on the edge and pulled on her flippers. Easing herself into the warm water, she momentarily forgot Michael and all her problems as the beauty and tranquility of the sea claimed her.

Taking a breath, she sank beneath the water and was lost to the delights of the ocean. The sun illuminated the coral reef, the unusual formations bright yellow in the day's light. The colorful tropical fish that lived in its shelter darted here and there, bright yellow, deep blue, fiery red. They swam tantalizingly near, only to skim away when her outstretched fingers came too close.

Katie lost track of time as she swam and enjoyed the beauty so recently discovered. Occasionally she'd see the shadow of another swimmer, but for the most part she was alone in the sunlight. The delicate beauty of the living coral reef was a constant source of delight to her, its intricate beauty endlessly fascinating. The water was clear, the sun illuminated the soft rose pinks and yellows of the coral. Sea anemones flowered in splendid pinks and blues, their dainty arms moving in the ocean currents as if they were waving to her.

Turning away from the reef at last, she sought the different species of fish that hugged its shelter. Many she recognized from previous dives, including the bright yellow and blue ones she didn't know the names of; the graceful angel-fish; the tiger-striped ones; the small silver darts.

Surfacing from time to time to keep track of the boat and the time, she enjoyed the afternoon.

At last, tired and happy, she slowly swam over to the boat and pulled herself up. Alone on the platform, she removed her mask and flippers and, sitting back, dangled her feet in the water. It was peaceful rocking gently with the boat, enjoying the warmth of the air on her cooled skin, her feet swishing in the tropical sea, listening to the murmur of the people on board, and watching the sun glisten on the water.

A time for peace, a time for dreaming. She let her eyes drift to the far horizon, her mind pleasantly drifting.

Another diver surfaced and swam towards the platform. Katie watched as he drew near; it was Michael. She scanned the surrounding water. Where was Elizabeth? Would she be next?

He pulled himself up beside her, water streaming from his tanned skin. She smiled shyly at him as he drew off his mask.

'Are you enjoying yourself?' he asked, grinning back.

'Yes, it's great.'

'It's remarkable. I've never seen anything like it. I think I'd like to try scuba, and go deeper, stay down longer.'

'Me, too. One day.' She turned to look back over the water. She felt content, at peace. She'd not get mad at Michael today.

'When's your next day off?' he asked her.

'Next Tuesday and Wednesday.'

'We could try it then.'

She looked over at him, then glanced back over the water. 'Where's Elizabeth?'

He smiled and looked out over the water as well.

'On the boat, I think. She didn't want to go diving- she wouldn't go scuba-diving.'

'So no conditions, and no others next time?'

'Does Elizabeth worry you?' Michael countered, slanting her a glance, his eyes narrowed against the sun's glare.

'No, should she?' Katie gazed out over the sparkling water, hoping he couldn't see the flush she felt rising at the lie.

'Elizabeth is no business of yours at all.'

Feeling snubbed, Katie fell silent. Her desire to learn scuba diving vied with her desire to stay away from this disturbing man.

Two others from the boat approached the platform and Michael and Katie stood up, moving to give them room.

'Michael, how was your swim?' Elizabeth, lounging on the deck of the boat, sat up when she saw him, smiling at first, but her face losing its appeal when she saw Katie beside him. 'Was it fascinating?' she added.

'You should have gone, Elizabeth—it was quite spectacular.'

He climbed to the back deck and went to sit beside her. Katie waited a moment, then climbed aboard herself, moving as far away from them as the limited space would permit.

She fell into conversation with a young couple from Ohio and sat with them during the cruise back to the dock.

Once in port, she was reluctant to approach Michael, but good manners dictated she thank him for her afternoon. It had been enjoyable for the most part and she would not give him the satisfaction of knowing that for her it was anything less than perfect.

She was one of the last off the boat, and followed the rest towards the hotel. Michael and the Bowman's were near the lobby and Katie quickened her pace. She knew the management's views of the staff using the hotel facilities, and didn't want to cause any trouble.

'Michael!' she called, hurrying to catch up.

He paused, spoke briefly to the Bowman's, then turned and started back towards her. They met after a few yards. Katie checked to make sure the lovely Elizabeth wasn't waiting before she spoke to him.

'Thank you for the snorkeling. It was such a pleasure. I'm glad you asked me.'

'Small enough thing, but I'm glad you enjoyed it.' He stood silently before her, watching her through his dark eyes. She stared back, trying to read his expression. It was hopeless; he gave nothing away.

'Well, I just wanted to say thank you,' she said.

'Next Tuesday?'

'What?'

'Scuba lessons next Tuesday?'

'I don't know if I can...' She tried to remember how much money she had in her bank account. Her job didn't pay much and it was proving more expensive than she had ever imagined just to live, especially on her salary. It had been a revelation to her that people really had to manage their money carefully. It was not something she'd had much experience with.

'Invite Jim if you want,' Michael broke in on her thoughts.

She blinked up at him. 'Why ever would I want to invite Jim? If anyone would like to come it would be Debbie and Rick.'

'Thought you and Jim...'

'You did not. I told you he was only a friend,' she reminded him.

'You want a recommendation for him.'

'Not on your terms. Blast it, Michael, the day was going nicely until you brought that up.'

'At least I can gauge how strongly you want help for Jim by the terms.'

'I don't care if you never help him!' she protested.

'You're turning into a feisty thing, Katie. I think I like it.' He leaned over, pausing scant inches from her mouth. 'But don't push your luck, young lady.'

Katie remained perfectly still, yearning for the touch of his lips on hers, anticipating the moment that never came.

Michael straightened, one eyebrow lifted in sardonic amusement. 'See you Tuesday.'

He turned and walked away. Katie watched him leave with a sudden, sickening realization. She loved him! She didn't want him to walk away; she wanted him to stay. She wanted him to walk by her side, be with her, for the two of them to build a life together. These last few weeks had shown her a different man from the one she married—or was he only different from the man he'd become over the last few years?

She loved the man she was growing to know.

But it was too late. She had made her position clear; there was no room for doubt. Over and over she'd been adamant she wanted a divorce. And at long last Michael had believed her and looked elsewhere.

Now what was she to do?

8

The blinding realization hit Katie hard. She stared after Michael for long moments before she slowly turned and started numbly walking home. How could she have been so foolish as to end their marriage? They had not spoken of love in years. But she knew she loved him. She had loved him when she married him, with an overwhelming love, a feeling of delight in his presence, awe that a man of his caliber should want her.

But how did Michael feel? Did he have any feelings for her beyond pride at the great hostess she proved to be?

Dare she tell him she'd changed her mind, that she no longer wanted a divorce.

She recoiled from such a step. He would laugh at her—laugh at her and tell her she was too late. Adamant about ending their marriage, she was now changing her mind because of—what?

Because I realized I love you. It sounded weak. Would he scoff, brush aside her discovery as of no importance? Which it could be to him. Especially if his emotions were now engaged with Elizabeth.

Katie was confused. How could she change her mind so drastically in so short a time? She had been unhappy in her marriage for years. Never overtly—just missing what she felt should be part of a marriage. Now, out on her own, surrounded by people she liked, doing things she wanted to do, she'd suddenly discovered that one of the things she loved was Michael Donovan. But not the husband of Boston—the man she saw here on Key West. Was it an illusion? A temporary aberration? Or had he changed?

She remembered his determination, his strength of purpose his focus with business. He'd made it big in a tough industry not by letting others dictate to him, but by going after what he wanted with a singleness of purpose.

Should she try the same technique? What if he didn't want her any more? What if she made a fool of herself over him?

It wouldn't be any different from the last few months. You've been a fool all along! The refrain echoed in her head as she walked slowly home.

Oblivious to the people around her, the bright, colorful shops and window displays, Katie walked along as if in a daze. The discovery of her feelings, so new and fragile, was stunning. She wanted to hide away and examine them closely. Determine what she really wanted, and what she should do.

Passing the street leading to her apartment, she continued until she reached the beach. Kicking off her sandals, she threaded her way through the sunbathers and found a quiet spot to the side. Sinking down on the hot sand, she gazed out at the shimmery water as if seeking an answer.

Each time she'd been with Michael on Key West replayed itself in her mind—from the unexpected first sight of him when she went to clean his room, to the picnic at the beach, dinner at the pizza parlor, breakfast in her kitchen. She should have realized where it was leading. She was always drawn to him, though trying to push him away, thinking she wanted to be free of him.

He was so different here from the self-contained man she'd known in Boston. Why hadn't she seen it before? Why hadn't she agreed to try it again with him when he'd suggested it? If he was willing to give up some of his business time, what else would she want? If he mentioned it again, she'd leap at the chance.

But would he ask again? Had he given up and turned his interests to Elizabeth?

She sat on the beach until darkness fell. Then, still dazed, she rose and slowly walked home. Heating soup for dinner, Katie felt no closer to a solution than she had when she first realized she still loved him. She longed to be with him, to see him again, longed to have him talk to her, put his arms around her; share himself with her, ask after her. What was she to do?

She was still in a dilemma the next morning. A fitful night's sleep had not helped, and she awoke feeling tired and depressed. She went for her morning swim, anxious to see Michael, hoping he'd be on the beach. Disappointment flooded through her when she reached the beach: it was empty and he didn't appear the entire time she stayed there.

Work was a chore for the first time since she'd arrived in Key West. She went through the motions, worried and upset. She wanted to see Michael, talk to him, find out how he viewed things. Had Elizabeth Bowman's arrival on the scene changed everything? Was it too late for reconciliation?

She paused at the window at the end of the hall, the one that overlooked the pool area. Spotting Michael lying back on one of the loungers, Katie stared down at him for long moments, delighting in the sight of his body, long and lean, muscular without being fat. He was growing quite tanned and it enhanced his sexy good looks. He was a man's man—authoritative, competent and self-assured. She'd never seen him at a loss. He always knew what to do, what he wanted.

Yet he could be charming, when it suited him. Katie remembered all the women who had hung on his every word at the various functions they'd attended. She'd never worried about him being unfaithful—he'd been too involved in business. But had he wanted he would have had no trouble finding willing women.

Her eyes were drawn to the woman on the next chair and her heart sank. Elizabeth. Here was another one more than willing to spend time with him. And, for the first time, someone Michael liked spending time with.

Katie turned to resume her work, an ache in her heart that wouldn't abate.

Twice more during the morning she was drawn to the window, watching for several moments each time. Wishing she had handled things differently. She wanted to be the one with Michael, enjoying the beauty of the day, talking together about inconsequential things, just spending time with him. She wanted him to laugh with her, and have him listen to her with the attention he showed Elizabeth.

She checked her watch. It was almost lunchtime. Would they eat by the pool or return to their rooms to change before going elsewhere? If the latter, Katie could talk to Michael for a moment. Use the excuse of the scuba trip as a reason to start talking. See what might develop.

She cleaned another room and darted to the window. They were still on the chairs. Two more rooms, two more trips to the window. This time Elizabeth was pulling on her cover-up, while Michael was talking with her father. It looked as if they were coming in.

Without thinking, Katie ascended to the higher floor and walked quickly to room 1124, Michael's room on this visit, according to Debbie. Using her passkey, she glanced both ways along the hall, then opened the door, closing it behind her. Debbie had already cleaned the room, and the sliding door to the balcony was left slightly ajar to permit the cool ocean breeze to freshen the room.

Nervously, Katie paced the carpet, pausing by the sliding door to gaze out over the various shades of blue water that comprised the Gulf of Mexico. Her heart pounded as tension rose within her. What would he say? What would she say?

'... me long, so I can meet you,' Michael broke off as he opened the door and saw Katie standing by the window. She turned to meet his gaze, startled to find Elizabeth beside him. Her eyes darted back to Michael, color staining her cheeks. Katie had not anticipated the other woman's presence.

He turned to Elizabeth. 'I'll meet you there about one.'

Elizabeth looked beyond him to Katie, her lips tight with anger. 'Will that give you enough time to change?' she bit out.

'I'll meet you at one, Elizabeth,' he said gently, stepping into the room and closing the door. Turning, he looked quizzically at Katie.

'And to what do I owe this honor?' he asked.

Now that she was facing him, her excuse seemed flimsy. She should have waited until she ran into him somewhere. Too late now—she was committed. She wiped her palms on her skirt.

'I—er—thought I could talk to you about—um— Tuesday.' She nervously adjusted the lamp on the table. When she glanced at him, his eyes were narrowed as if in assessment. She swallowed hard. This was not as easy as she had thought it would be.

He stepped into the room and tossed his towel on his bed. He wore only sandals and his swimming trunks. His shoulders were broad and brown, his chest firm, muscular, his legs long and dark beneath his swimsuit. His skin was evenly tanned, dark and rich. Gone was the pink he'd acquired that first day. He looked as if he belonged outdoors.

She swallowed, her heart filled with longing and desire. His dark hair was wind-blown and disheveled, strongly appealing. Her fingers longed to brush it from his forehead. She tried to breathe. How could she have thought she didn't love this man?

She ached to be with him, do things for him, ached for him to ask her to rub lotion on his skin again. Her hands tingled in anticipation. She yearned to lie beside him at the pool or at the beach. She clenched her fists and turned away. She couldn't think while looking at him, only experience a terrifying desire that threatened to swamp her.

'I was going to contact you about the scuba lessons,' he said easily, moving quietly across the room to stand beside her. Gently, he turned her around. He was so close. She looked up to meet his eyes, unaware of the confusion and longing that she showed. His gaze set her senses tingling. Desire rose rampant through her whole body; she longed to reach out to touch him, feel the warmth of his skin, the strength beneath, have his hands touch her again, experience once more of his hot kisses on a tropical day.

'We're on for Tuesday. Meet at the dock at 7:30 in the morning. Is that all?' he asked softly, a satisfied look on his face. 'I'm due to meet Elizabeth and her father for lunch.'

She dropped her eyes, desperately longing for something to say that would keep him with her, something that would lead to more time together.

'I wouldn't want to keep you from lunch with Elizabeth,' she said bitterly. 'Does she know you're the head of Donovan Construction?'

'Yes, she does, but I think she likes me for myself. I think she enjoys spending time with me,' he replied.

'I like to spend time with you.' Her voice was so soft, she wasn't sure he heard her.

He chuckled softly, tilting her chin up with his finger. His eyes danced down at hers, and her heart tripped faster.

'You have a funny way of showing it, Katie— always telling me to go away, and how you long for a divorce. Excuse me for not realizing how much you wanted to be with me.' A hint of his hardness crept into his speech.

Shame flushed her face and she licked her lips. Her chin burned from his touch and she dropped her gaze to his lips, longing for his kiss.

'You once said you'd never let me go,' she said softly, clinging to his hard words of the other morning.

'People say things in anger they wouldn't otherwise say,' was the reply.

Her heart sank. 'You didn't mean it?'

He sighed and released her, moving towards his wardrobe to pull out some shorts and a clean shirt.

'Katie, did you come here to rehash a statement made when I was angry, or what? I need to change for lunch.'

He stepped into the bathroom and a minute later Katie heard the shower. She moved to the balcony and sat on the edge of the chair there, blind to the beauty of the island, her thoughts on the man in the shower. The conversation was not going the way she wanted it, but at least he hadn't kicked her out.

The shower ceased and she held her breath. Letting it out slowly, she tried to calm her jumpy nerves. Endless moments of time spun by, then she heard his step behind her. When she looked, he was ready for lunch. His hair had been neatly combed, and his tan was shown off by the choice of clothes he wore.

'I liked your hair better messed up,' she said involuntarily.

'So mess it up,' he invited, sitting on the chair adjacent to hers.

Some impulse of mischief took hold and Katie rose and

ruffled his hair, which was still damp from his shower. She stood up and admired the effect, a saucy grin on her face.

He laughed and pulled her down into his lap, one hand around her back, the other resting just beneath her breast. Katie's breath was knocked out from her with the unexpected action. Her face was only inches from Michael's and she gazed into his eyes, lost to all thought except his nearness, how much she loved him and how she had messed things up.

Boldly she encircled his neck, her fingers tangled in the damp hair at the nape. Her other hand rested on his chest, just above his heart. She could feel the slow, rhythmic beat. Dependable, steady. Like Michael himself.

'What do you want, Katie?' he asked, his eyes holding hers.

'I don't know,' she whispered back, unable to look away, unable to voice her feelings, unable to tell him what she longed to say. He'd think her such an idiot. And she wasn't brave enough to risk his rejection.

'Maybe you should find out what you want.' His voice was sharp, his eyes glittered into hers. But his touch belied his look. His hand moved and slowly began to unbutton the front of her uniform, his fingers brushing gently against the soft skin hidden by the cotton dress.

Katie trembled in his arms as the dress began to fall away. She wore no bra beneath her work clothes, and Michael's touch and intentions were clear. Warmth spread through her when his hand reached her waist and one finger trailed up the shadowy valley exposed by the open dress. Gently he spread the material from her breasts.

His eyes dropped from hers to the satiny skin he was stroking, from her shoulder across the swell of her breast, into the valley between. Katie closed her eyes in exquisite delight at the feel of his roughened fingertips caressing her. Softly they moved back and forth, then down the mound to the tip, circling it, before moving back up towards her shoulders. Then he started again. Her skin quivered and danced beneath his touch, aching to feel his skin against hers, the trails of exquisite passion pervading, her body growing warm as she yearned for him to continue.

She could scarcely breathe; the emotions and sensations caused by his touch were almost overwhelming. Trembling, she was afraid to move, afraid to break the spell, to end this magical moment.

'You have always been so beautiful,' he murmured.

Katie's eyes flew open to meet his. His warm palm took the weight of her breast, his thumb teased the nipple, but his eyes never left hers and Katie could see the hunger reflected in them.

Did it reflect the hunger she knew must be on her own face? Daringly she moved fractionally closer, her lips parted to meet his, her breath mingling with his, the heat in her body owing nothing to the heat of the day, but only to Michael, his proximity, his nearness, his touch.

The sharp rap on the door shattered the moment. Stunned, Katie pulled back, her eyes wide, seeking the source of the noise. She sat up and pulled her dress closed, refusing to meet Michael's eyes.

'Michael? Are you in there?' Elizabeth's voice called imperatively.

He glanced at his watch.

'Damn! I told her I'd meet her at one and now it's ten after.' Unceremoniously he set Katie on her feet and rose. Brushing his fingers through his hair, he tried to bring some order to it.

'Elizabeth, I'll be right there.' He looked at Katie. 'What do I do with you?' he murmured, shaking his head. Crossing to the bathroom he disappeared inside, returning in only a moment with his hair neatly combed.

Stepping to the corner of the balcony, hidden from the room by the drapes that covered the inside of the windows, Katie quickly refastened her dress. Her breathing was fast, her heart beating in double time. Leaning against the wall that separated the balconies, she closed her eyes, hoping Elizabeth wouldn't see her.

Hearing the door close, she paused for a long moment, ears straining for sounds in the room. She heard no voices. Slowly she peeked around. The room was empty. Feeling very much the scarlet woman, Katie walked slowly to the door, hesitating before opening it a crack. She didn't want to find them waiting at the elevator. Peering out into the hall, she saw no one, so she slipped through the door, closed it firmly behind her and headed for the stairs.

At least he hadn't kicked her out. But he had left her for Elizabeth. She frowned; she didn't think she'd progressed at all. She needed to talk to him, but not around other people. Maybe on the scuba-dive.

Katie had almost finished changing into her own clothes when Debbie pushed her cart in. She waited for her friend, not wanting to be alone with her thoughts another afternoon, and wanting some activities to take her mind off things.

'Marlise is going shopping—she wants some new curtains for her place; want to go?' Debbie asked as she changed.

'Sure do; I'll look for some things, too.' Katie's heart wasn't in it, but it would help pass the time and maybe it could help raise her spirits.

'How was the snorkeling yesterday?' Debbie asked as they left.

'Wonderful.' Katie could scarcely remember the pleasure she had found at the reef, the events since having overshadowed everything else. Had it only been yesterday that her discovery had turned her world upside-down?

'I want to go to that fabric store over on Simonton Street. I'm making some new curtains and want to get some fabric,' Marlise said, when Katie and Debbie met her in front of the gift shop.

'Whatever, we're just along for the ride,' Debbie said. 'Right, Katie?'

'Yes.' Katie's eyes scanned the lobby, seeing if she could spot Michael or Elizabeth Bowman. Neither was in sight. She didn't really expect to see them. The attractions of Key West were not found in the lobbies of hotels.

They walked the couple of blocks to the factory that produced lovely colorful fabrics used for dresses, shirts, curtains, and upholstery. The colors were bright, the designs bold and exciting. Other visits had been pleasurable for Katie; today, however, she was listless and lethargic. She tried to follow the conversation between the other two, but her thoughts kept dwelling on her own problems.

'Look at this!' Marlise held up a bolt of material in a beautiful pink, with various shadings delineating large tropical leaves. It was soft cotton, and quite expensive. 'Wish I had the money to buy it. I need yards and yards, though. It's too much.' She looked through other racks, talking casually. 'Wish I had the money your friend Michael must have, Katie.'

Katie's attention was immediately caught, and held. 'What makes you say that?' she asked.

'He must have plenty. He bought a bracelet from the gift shop this afternoon. It was beautiful and not inexpensive. He just wrote a check for it.'

'For the voluptuous Miss Bowman?' Debbie asked, throwing a glance at Katie.

'Well, I guess so; who else? She was in with him and they were looking over things. He came back some time later and bought the bracelet—one of those gold ones that are all little conch-shells; do you know which ones I mean?'

Katie nodded, the constriction in her throat preventing speech. She knew which one—small, delicate, utterly beautiful. The conch-shell was the emblem of Key West. The bracelet Marlise mentioned was delicately wrought of gold. Katie had seen it several times, admired it, and now Michael had bought it for Elizabeth.

Her spirits dropped. Something that expensive was not a trifle to be bought for a casual friend.

'Well, money likes money, and now that Elizabeth has appeared on the scene we don't see much of Michael,' Debbie commented. 'Though Katie went snorkeling with them yesterday.'

'Tell us, Katie, are they an item? How did they behave?' Marlise's eyes sparkled with romantic thoughts.

'It's hard to say,' Katie said slowly. 'I guess I would have thought them friends.'

Debbie nodded. 'Good breeding—they aren't going to show their feelings in public.'

'So that means you and Rick don't have good breeding?' Marlise teased. 'You're always holding hands and sneaking kisses when you think no one is looking.'

'Nothing of the sort. Anyway, I think it's too soon to see much between Michael and Miss Bowman—they just met a few days ago. And before that I always thought our Michael was making a play for Katie.' Debbie glanced at Katie again.

Katie looked up at both pairs of eyes fixed on her, awaiting her reaction. She shrugged. 'Guess not. Look at this material, Marlise. Don't you love it?'

She was desperate to change the subject. She did not want to have to talk about Michael and Elizabeth. The main reason she came this afternoon was to escape thoughts of the two of them, not to end up discussing them.

The outing wasn't working. Katie patiently waited until Marlise had found her material and purchased it, then excused herself from the rest of the afternoon.

'I've got some grocery shopping I need to get done,' she explained.

Debbie looked at her with a funny expression, but said nothing. They parted at the corner of Duval and Green Street, Marlise and Debbie to hunt up other friends at JoJos, and Katie to head towards home and the shopping she claimed awaited her.

Duval Street was alive with people shopping, sightseeing and stopping for refreshments at the various outdoor cafes that dotted the street. Katie wove in and out of the people heading towards Mallory Square and the nightly sunset festivities. Their happiness and excitement only emphasized her own loneliness and confusion. She'd buy her groceries and have a quiet night, she decided. After the wakeful one before, she would relish an early night.

'Katie.' A familiar voice from one of the sidewalk café tables called.

Katie stopped and looked around. Elizabeth Bowman beckoned from under an umbrella. She had a colorful drink in front of her and several bags on the chair beside her. She appeared to be alone. Katie hesitated a moment, then walked towards her.

'Have a seat.' The dark-haired woman gestured to the empty chair at her table. 'I wanted a chance to talk to you—I'm glad I saw you passing.'

Katie pulled out the chair and sat down, her eyes wary as she looked at Elizabeth. She wasn't sure this was wise. She wished she hadn't left the security of her friends.

Elizabeth gave a nervous little laugh. 'This is more awkward than I anticipated. For your own good I felt I should speak to you. You mustn't misconstrue the attentions of the guests in the hotel, you know.'

Katie stared at her, suspecting exactly where she was leading, but wondering how far she would actually go. Did Michael have any idea Elizabeth was talking to her she wondered.

'Guests are often friendly with the hotel help. You live here, you can advise us where the best places are to shop, or swim or eat. In exchange for that kind of advice some guests may treat the hotel staff to an outing or give a larger tip. Do you understand what I'm talking about?' Elizabeth floundered.

Katie's eyes danced with suppressed amusement, but she solemnly shook her head. This was Elizabeth's show; let her run it.

'You're making a fool of yourself over Michael Donovan!' Elizabeth snapped, losing all patience. 'I doubt the hotel would look kindly on a maid who abused the privilege of her master key to let herself into a guest's room uninvited and sat waiting for his return.'

Katie's eyes widened slightly, but she remained silent. Miss Bowman was very correct in her assessment and it would not do to have her report her to the management of the hotel. But she refused to let the woman know that that threat had any power.

'Dammit, stay away from Michael Donovan!' Elizabeth stormed, losing her temper completely.

Katie sat up straight in her chair and said in a soft voice, 'I have known Michael Donovan for a long time. I have never known him to have others fight his battles for him. If he finds me an embarrassment, he will certainly let me know. He doesn't need someone else doing it for him. I think it's you who are embarrassed by my being around, Miss Bowman.'

She stood up and looked down at the dark-haired woman.

'When Michael tells me to stay away, I will. Good afternoon.' And with her head held high, Katie left the small cafe and continued down Duval Street.

Would Elizabeth tell Michael of their encounter? One day soon he'd probably tell her he didn't want to see her, Katie, again. But until then, Elizabeth wouldn't have the last word.

She didn't know how she'd bear it if he told her that. But she'd find a way. She had pushed for the divorce, not Michael.

When she reached home, after stopping at the neighborhood market for a few things, she was surprised to find a letter awaiting her. She rarely got mail, unless it was the notice for monthly rent. The return address indicated O'Mally, Evans and Stuart—the lawyers handling her divorce.

A wave of nausea washed through her, and her hands began to tremble. Did this contain the final papers? Michael had said it would take a few months.

Entering the apartment, she went to the kitchen, carefully putting away the few groceries she had purchased. She poured herself a glass of iced tea and sat down, letter in hand. For a long time she stared at it. Addressed to her in elegant typeset, the prestigious Boston return address embossed on the envelope did nothing but cause a myriad of conflicting thoughts to crowd in.

Finally, with a sigh of resignation, she slit the envelope and slowly withdrew the paper. It was a letter. As she read it, her shock grew. It was not the final divorce papers—that process was moving along. What shocked her was the last paragraph:

And, per the instructions of Mr. Michael Donovan, we are contacting you to ascertain if there are any personal items in the property that you wish to have before the property is sold. Your personal effects, clothes, jewels and make-up will be forwarded to the address of your choosing. Our client also asked us to forward any other items of your choosing to the aforementioned address.

Michael was selling the house!

She was stunned. Tears welled in her eyes, spilled over and ran unheeded over her cheeks. She remembered his bringing her to it when they were first married. Remembered him showing off all the beautiful furnishings with almost boyish pride. She'd found it impressive and cold, like a museum, but in those days she'd had such high hopes to change it, fill it with love and laughter and children. He loved that house. It represented the long hard climb he'd made from the childhood he'd had to success.

However, none of the things she had longed for at the time of their marriage had happened. For years it had merely been a place to eat and sleep.

She had never liked it, but it had been her home for seven years. Michael's pride and joy.

Now it was gone. As their life together was gone. This, more than anything else, showed her their marriage was truly over.

How like Michael to plunge ahead without consulting her, without even notifying her. He'd spoken with her a dozen times, yet never mentioned selling the house. He hadn't changed after all. He was still ruthless, and hard, and quick to make decisions that suited him—paying no attention to anyone else.

She gazed dully into space.

She knew him. Despite it all, she still longed for him with an intensity that was startling.

Katie sat a long time at the table, reviewing their life together, trying to see where she should have done things differently, could have done things differently. Darkness fell, and still she sat, the letter in front of her, her tea forgotten and the tears dried on her face.

She was homesick. Now that it was too late, far too late, a fierce homesickness welled up and threatened to overwhelm her. She wanted the familiarity of her house, her acquaintances, her committee work and the streets of Boston that she knew so well. She wanted to see her aunt, hear her lecture on Katie's duty and responsibilities in the old society that was Boston.

But most of all she wanted to be with Michael when he met people; watch him work at the business he did so well; be proud of him for his accomplishments and have him be proud of her for what she could contribute.

Feeling a hundred years old, she rose and switched on the lights, getting paper and pen. Writing first to the attorneys and then to her aunt, Katie arranged her future. She wanted nothing from the house, her clothes could go to her aunt's place, and she would decide later which, if any, she wanted sent on to her at Key West.

She felt old, tired and drained. Her newfound freedom mocked her. She didn't want it. She wanted Michael. Her dislike for her old life faded. Seeing Michael again, she longed to return with him. Their lives had changed; she had changed enough so that she could make their future different from the past. Their life together would be different now, would be so enriched just by their being together.

Except that she had thrown it away. And now there was Elizabeth. Michael gave no indication he wanted to resume their life, no indication that he wanted to see Katie at all. He seemed quite taken with Elizabeth.

Just before she went to bed, Katie remembered their outing on Tuesday. She'd have that to look forward to. Could she bring the conversation around to themselves, lead him to reveal his feelings, see if he would want to try again?

Or would it be their last time together?

9

Tuesday morning Katie awoke with mixed expectations. Would she and Michael get along or be at cross-purposes all day? She'd been looking forward to the day since her meeting with Elizabeth. If that woman was not sure of Michael, maybe Katie was wrong in thinking he was interested in her.

She hoped he'd meant it when he said Elizabeth wouldn't be accompanying them. Surely he couldn't be totally taken with her if he left her behind today.

Katie hadn't seen him in person—just from the hall window when he was lying by the pool. Once or twice she thought he'd seen her at the window, but she couldn't be sure. She'd stepped back quickly each time, yet again and again was drawn to the scene by the pool. She ached with loneliness and longing. Her heart ached watching him enjoy himself with someone else. Yet unable to stop herself from gazing at him.

She dressed in a brief two-piece turquoise swimsuit. Pulling on a matching cover-up that came to the tops of her thighs, she put her snorkeling equipment, sunscreen and towels in her tote. She was ready.

A knock sounded on the door. Opening it wide, she smiled involuntarily when she saw Michael. Her relief was almost tangible. She'd been worried all week he'd call with an excuse to cancel the excursion.

He wore faded denim shorts, an old cotton shirt opened to

the waist—and he looked as if he'd combed his hair with an egg-beater.

'I like your hairstyle.' She grinned up at him, the day suddenly perfect.

His eyes were smiling as he reached out to draw his fingers down her cheek. 'I thought you would. Ready?'

'Yes.'

'Did you eat?'

'A while ago.' She didn't want him to know she'd been up since five in anticipation of their day.

'Good,' he said as she picked up her tote. He escorted her to the taxi he had waiting. Katie slid across the back seat to the opposite door and placed her bag on the seat between her and Michael. Looking at him shyly, she didn't know what to make of his picking her up; she could have met him at the dock.

He climbed in, moved the bag to the floor and pulled Katie closer to him. She looked startled, but made no comment. How could she? Her heart was in her throat. The heat from Michael's body, scant inches from her own, generated electrical impulses that sparked currents of delight throughout her being. While she kept her eyes firmly to the front, every inch of her concentrated on the man beside her. Her nerve-endings quivered for his touch and it took great restraint to prevent herself from flinging herself into his arms.

The cab drove to Front Street, and pulled up near the pier where the sleek white diving boat awaited. It was the same boat they had sailed on last week for the snorkel trip. When Katie climbed aboard, she looked for the other passengers. Were they early?

Once Michael had joined her, the skipper cast off and the big boat headed for the coral reef. 'Are we the only ones?' Katie asked as they got under way.

'Yes. I chartered the boat for the day, for the two of us. I understand we can only dive for short periods of time, with a couple of hours' rest in between, so I wanted us to get the most out of the day,' Michael explained as he sat near her on the bench seat.

Spray from the bow blew gently across them as the boat headed crossways to the breeze from the Gulf. The sky was a deep clear blue, the water only a shade darker. The air caressed them as the breeze tried to outrun the boat.

Katie discarded her cover-up and felt the warmth from the sun kiss her skin. It felt wonderful. She loved Key West and its climate. She was looking forward to learning how to scuba-dive.

She glanced over and saw Michael's gaze on her. She smiled shyly and looked back towards the bow. He moved to sit beside her, one hand trailing across her ribs. Her heart jumped, began beating again.

'Have you lost weight?' he asked over the muffled roar of the engines.

She shook her head, refusing to answer. That would give rise to questions and speculation—to confessions she was not willing to make.

'Well, you're too thin, then,' he said in her ear.

She turned; his face was mere inches from hers. 'I think it comes from being more active down here.' Her voice trailed off as his lips descended on hers.

His lips were demanding, the kiss intense. To her it was glorious. She turned to face him, open to his kiss, wanting to give him as much delight as he was giving her, her mouth moving beneath his, her tongue reaching out to taste him, feel his mouth open, draw her in. The pounding of the heavy diesel engines matched the pounding in her ears as she lost track of time. Did the kiss last for long endless moments, or eons? Was the erotic touch of his tongue and lips a dream or reality?

Heat and desire and longing arose, warred and crashed over her. His mouth evoked waves of delight, pleasures remembered from other kisses on Key West, learned but recently, and longed for endlessly.

Katie reached out her hand to touch his shoulder, but Michael broke contact, carefully setting her away from him. His eyes gazed down into hers as he moved back a couple of feet, putting distance between them.

'You're too dangerous. We're here to learn to scuba dive, nothing more.'

Katie's eyes mirrored the hurt and bewilderment his rejection caused. She turned slowly to face the front, her shoulders drooping slightly. Had he remembered Elizabeth? Was that the reason to stop?

She'd bring all the pride of her family to front and show him he could not daunt a Harrington. She had often played a role when hostessing for him; she could do it one more time.

When the boat reached the reef, the skipper and his assistant instructed Michael and Katie on how to use the scuba equipment, how to dive, and what to watch for while diving. Each person was responsible for donning his or her own gear, but the partner had to check it to make sure it was on securely and correctly. This was demonstrated for them, then they had to do it for each other.

Katie double-checked Michael's straps, making sure they weren't twisted, and were securely fastened. She had to stand close to him, and her hands fluttered against his shoulders as she tested the belt, the warmth from his skin adding to the warmth she felt from the sun. Her heart pounded as she remembered their kiss. She wished he hadn't ended it.

When she was satisfied, he checked hers, his fingers slipping beneath the straps on her shoulders to verify they were not too tight, moving slowly inside the strap, brushing lightly against her heated skin, causing her to forget the lesson, forget the others on the boat and seek his eyes. Her body felt as malleable as soft rubber and she swayed towards him, her eyes alight. He gazed back at her, then he turned abruptly away, a frown on his face.

Katie turned away feeling foolish. She had to concentrate on what they were being taught, not imagine an interest that wasn't there. This might be her only chance to learn to scuba-dive. She'd make the most of it.

But she couldn't help her eyes flickering to Michael from time to time, and on each occasion his eyes met hers, his gaze giving nothing away. She couldn't hear the captain, couldn't feel the breeze, nor hear the soft murmur of the water against the hull of the ship. She could only feel the pull of attraction, the longing that filled her in his presence.

At last it was time to practice what they'd been taught. All tension slipped away as Katie slipped beneath the warm water. She loved scuba diving instantly. It was better than snorkeling because she didn't have to surface. They went deeper than she had ever gone before, though not too many feet down on the first dive. The captain's assistant accompanied them, pointing out the reef nearby. The coral formations were even more beautiful at the deeper level than near the surface. The water stayed clear and pristine and she could see for yards in every direction, delighting in the beauty of the sea.

Reluctant to surface when the diving instructor indicated it was time, she broke the water first and looked around for Michael. When his head broke through, she could see his smile, even behind the mouthpiece.

Once on board, Katie was quick to talk to the captain about how much fun it was and the differences immediately apparent from snorkeling. Michael watched with indulgent eyes, sharing her enthusiasm, watching Katie endlessly.

After a hearty lunch served on the aft deck, Katie leaned back in one of the loungers.

'I may never move again,' she said drowsily. 'This is tiring work.'

'Time for another dive after the two-hour rest,' the captain asked.

She opened one eye and nodded. 'Count me in. But first a brief nap.'

'Come on, Katie, we'll take a turn on the bow.' Michael rose and reached out his hand for hers. She looked up, surprised, but quickly rose, taking his hand. He gathered up their towels and sunscreen and walked along the narrow side of the boat to the wide flat bow deck.

Spreading out their towels side by side, Michael dropped to his, rolling on to his chest.

'Spread the sunscreen on my back, would you?' he asked, his voice somewhat muffled.

Katie knelt beside him, pouring some of the lotion in her hands then spreading it across his back. It reminded her of the day they'd played volleyball. She enjoyed touching him, reveling in the feel of his warm skin beneath her fingers, the strong muscles, relaxed now but capable of strength he rarely used. His skin, smooth, dark, stretched tightly over his frame.

Gradually her touch changed as she watched him. It became more erotic. She used her nails to lightly trail down his back to his shorts, tracing the strong backbone, digging in slightly across his shoulders.

Without warning, Michael rolled on to his back and captured her wrists with his hands. His eyes narrowed against the glare of the sun, he studied her for a long moment. Katie smiled a slow, seductive smile at the man she loved.

'What the hell do you think you're doing?' he bit out.

'Spreading on lotion,' she replied innocently, her look bely-
ing her words. 'Shall I spread it on your chest?'

Michael was silent for a long moment, his tension rising till
it was almost tangible. Then he relaxed. 'No, I can manage that.
Turn about's only fair, though. Shall I put lotion on your back?'

She nodded and moved to pull away, but his hands tightened
on her wrists. Slowly, he pulled her hands apart, spreading their
arms until she lost balance and fell against his chest.

She watched as he smiled lazily and reached one hand
around to find the lotion and pour some on her back. Slowly his
hands smoothed the liquid over her skin, his fingers soothing
across her back, up to her shoulders as she lay across his chest.

With a quick motion, he unfastened the ties holding her top in
place and eased the spaghetti-straps from her shoulders. His hands
created patterns and whorls of delight across her sensitive skin.

Katie closed her eyes in pleasure. 'If I were a cat, I'd be purr-
ing now,' she whispered, dropping her cheek to rest against
Michael's. His hands continued their wandering, caressing her,
trailing fire and enchantment over her back.

He raised her up and her eyes flew open to meet his. Slowly,
deliberately, he removed the top of her swimsuit and then lowered her to rest against his chest.

Her breasts swelled with desire as her hot skin met his. Deep
within her Katie felt the hot stir of passion build. She gazed
down into his dark eyes, every inch of her being alive to his,
wanting more, longing for fulfillment that only Michael could
bring. Fulfillment long denied.

'Do you still feel like a cat?' he asked softly.

'No...'

She felt like a woman, alive, on the edge of a great discovery.

His hands moved to her sides, caressing the soft swell of her
breasts. One thumb pushed between to locate her nipple, to
bring it to throbbing awareness.

Katie was weak with pleasure, and hot flames licked deep within her in time to the pulse Michael brought with his touch. She moved her hips in the age-old movement, her eyes glazed with passion, her whole body, her whole being, caught up in his magical touch.

'Stop that, or I can't be held responsible,' he hissed in her ear. His mouth captured hers, his hand moving her head for his kiss, his fingers tangling in her short hair. His thumb continued its assault and Katie was lost.

The heat from the sun on her back mingled with the heat from Michael below her and her own fiery core. Blinding light from the sea, the sky and behind her lids illuminated life and the love she felt for this man. Dared she speak of it? Could she speak? Her whole body was entangled with his, caught up in sensations and pleasures. She throbbed in desire and yearning.

Could she capture this moment for all time? Never end it, never go back to loneliness, unhappiness, and heartache?

Michael sat up, hugging her close to his chest, catching her between that hard wall of muscle and his strong thighs. His hands petted her, soothed her as his strong arms held her tightly against him.

Then his grip loosened and he rested her against his legs, one finger tracing a rosy tip, his eyes devouring her. Her lips dry from his kisses, Katie licked them, drawing his eye.

'I want to kiss you all over, feel the softness of your lips, the hardness of your jaw, trail kisses down your throat, across the swell of your breast, take your nipple in my mouth and feel it grow hard against my lips, my tongue,' he murmured, and slowly his finger traced the point in question, rubbing gently, erotically.

Katie moaned softly as deep inside hunger grew for this man.

'Touch you where no one else has ever touched you but me,' he continued. 'Make you mine again and again. But not here, and not now. There're others around. When we make love, it will be alone, with none to see but ourselves.' His voice soothed her, while his hands inflamed her. She wanted to snuggle against him, seeking more, seeking fulfillment. Her hands entangled themselves in his hair and she tried to bring him to her.

'Easy, baby, easy does it.'

She pulled back, tears of frustration swimming in her eyes as she tried to see him. Emotions churned within her. Her body craved his, craved what he denied her, longed for what he refused to give her.

'Will we ever make love again, Michael?' she asked, longing clearly evident in her face, in her whole body.

He shook his head, looking beyond her to the bright, shiny sea. 'I don't know, Katie; you hold that key.'

She closed her eyes, the tears seeping from beneath her lids. Yes, if she slept with him, asked him the favor for Jim. She held the key, but to what unhappiness? He didn't want her? He didn't ask her for himself?

He held her until she stirred and pushed away, searching for her top. Without looking at him, she pulled it back on and refastened it, then she lay down on her towel, turned away from Michael and let the soothing rhythm of the rocking boat calm her. Tears fell silently on the deck, and before long she drifted off into an uneasy sleep.

The afternoon dive did not hold the enjoyment that the morning one had for Katie, and by the time they headed back towards Key West she had a raging headache. She'd practically thrown herself at him, and he had held her off. If she slept with him, he'd give Jim his recommendation. And then what? Go off with Elizabeth, knowing he'd won? Her head throbbed with tension. She longed for the privacy of her apartment.

Donning dark glasses, she sat apart from him on the ride back and counted the minutes until she could be alone again. A couple of aspirins and a glass of water— that was all she wanted right now.

When Katie saw Elizabeth waiting at the dock, it was the last straw. Anger flared against the woman, against Michael. Her head pounded with emotion and it was all Katie could do to be cordial.

'Thank you, Michael, for taking me diving,' she said stiffly, refusing to meet his eye. Blast the man anyway; why had he ever come to Key West? She had been happy during the months before he came. Now everything was different, changed. Her head throbbed, the sun dazzling against her eyes.

'The pleasure was mine today.' Was there hidden meaning in his words? She refused to look at him to see, fixing her eyes on the dock.

Katie didn't see the expression on Michael's face when he first saw Elizabeth; she didn't want to. She only wanted to get away. She stepped on to the dock as soon as the boat was moored. With head held high, she marched to the first cab in the queue, neither by word nor look acknowledging Elizabeth Bowman's presence.

She felt as if she were holding her breath. Any movement and she would let go and explode. But it was only her tenuous control over her emotions. Soon she'd be in the privacy of her apartment and could relax. If she cried, or screamed with rage, or threw things, there would be none to see. The pounding headache didn't abate. She longed for the coolness and peace of her apartment, away from her friends, away from Michael, away from the problems that now crowded against her, overwhelming her.

When the cab drew up to her home, Katie stared in surprise at her front porch. Beside two suitcases, in her splendid rose silk suit, complete with diamonds and pearls, waited her Aunt Margaret.

10

It was too much. Katie was too distraught over Michael to deal with her aunt now. She sat, stunned, in the back seat, feeling totally out of control. Slowly, she opened the car door. She had so wanted to be alone. She wasn't sure she was up to dealing with her aunt, hearing her lecture on Katie's proper place and duties and responsibilities. She wanted to be left alone. Was that too much to ask?

'Hello, Aunt Margaret,' Katie said formally, climbing the shallow steps and leaning forward to peck her on the cheek. 'I didn't know you were coming.'

'No, it was a surprise visit. Can you carry my bags?'

'Of course.' The older woman traveled light—there were only two small suitcases.

Margaret smiled at her niece regally, following her into her apartment. When Katie deposited her suitcases inside the door, she carefully closed it and turned to face her aunt.

'I received a rather disjointed letter from you, Katie, and decided I had better come down here and find out what is going on. What with your running off the way you did, and the very brief, uninformative phone conversations we had, I've been very worried about you,' Margaret Harrington said quietly.

'Oh, Aunt Margaret, I've made such a mess of things!'

With that, the cool, calm, serene, socially correct Katie Harrington-Donovan burst into tears.

Her astonished aunt could only stare. She hadn't seen her niece cry in over ten years, not since she was a young teenager. She had no idea how to handle the situation, and could only pat her shoulder and say, 'There, there, Katie. I'm sure it's not all that bad.'

'It is,' Katie assured her, tears not abating. Everything was just too much. She'd been a fool and now would have to live with the consequences for the rest of her life. She wanted Michael with a passion that was frightening, yet he turned from her and went to Elizabeth. She'd thought she'd known what she was doing, and had only proved she hadn't. The tears wouldn't stop.

Margaret rose and went to find the kitchen to prepare some tea. It had always worked in the past.

Ten minutes later she brought in two steaming cups, as Katie finally brought herself under control, lying back against the sofa, drained.

'Sorry, Aunt Margaret, but I'm so unhappy,' she said. The tissue was wadded in her hands, and tears still slipped through her lips, trailed down her cheeks.

'So it appears. Now, why don't you tell me all about it? Your letter was totally confusing, and then I get a call from some attorneys saying I'm to receive your property. Michael is selling the house?'

Katie nodded, tears welling again. She took a sip of the hot tea—anything to escape from the crying bout she couldn't seem to stop. Her heart ached, her head throbbed and the tears kept falling.

'Well, I'm sorry to hear it. It's a fine place, in such a good neighborhood.'

Katie giggled unexpectedly through her tears. How like her aunt to think of that. No thoughts to what her niece was going through. It wasn't funny, but her emotions were so raw, she couldn't help it.

Margaret looked disapproving. 'Make up your mind; is it funny or sad?'

'Both. Sad that I made such a botch of everything, but funny that you think only of things such as a good neighborhood.'

'Things like that are important,' Margaret said sharply.

Katie shook her head slowly, blotting the tears. She looked at her aunt through swollen eyes.

'No, I don't think they're important. What's important is being with the person you love. Helping that person, sharing with him, doing for him. Not the trappings of wealth, proper social places, or right neighborhoods. If Michael lived in a hovel, I'd still want to be with him.'

She trailed off sadly and took another sip of tea. Reaching for a tissue, she blew her nose and leaned back again, feeling drained and exhausted. And incredibly sad. Her heart ached, her whole body longed for the unattainable. She had never felt this way before, not even when contemplating leaving Michael. Not when she'd first left Boston. Would it ever fade, not be so painful, or would she carry this with her all her life?

Margaret was silent, sipping her tea, eyes taking in the cheerful home her niece had made for herself.

'You have made a nice place here, Katie. It's pleasant. Tell me what's happened.'

So Katie related her story, telling her aunt of the discontent she had felt in Boston, the neglect of her husband, the dreary rounds of charity events and business affairs.

She told her of coming to Key West, of how much she'd learned and grown, and of Michael's unexpected arrival.

'At first, I thought he was the same as ever—domineering, consumed by business. Even though he told me he would change, he didn't. When the office called, he dropped everything to respond.' She realized she'd been deeply hurt by his turning from her that night at the hotel, forsaking her for the call of business.

'But then he came back, he said he'd turned over the business to his managers and he would stay here with me.'

'Only you didn't want him,' her aunt said knowledgeably.

Katie nodded her head, took another sip of tea, her eyes on her cup.

'I thought I didn't. I was looking for something more than what we had these last few years. But then, he had changed. He seemed different. He wouldn't take no for an answer, kept coming around. Gradually I thought...' She trailed off. She hadn't thought anything until Elizabeth appeared on the scene and she realized she could really lose Michael.

'Well, what are you going to do about it?' Margaret asked.

'There's nothing I can do about it.'

'Nonsense. There's always something to be done. What do you want?'

Katie stared off into space. Michael had asked her the same question. She hadn't been sure enough to answer him then. Now she was.

'I want Michael.'

'Then go and get him.' Her aunt made it sound as easy as shopping for fish.

'He's met someone else.'

'Who?'

'Elizabeth Bowman.'

'Never heard of her,' her aunt sniffed.

'She's from New York.'

'That hardly matters. He came down here after you, Katie; you just said so. Though why he would I can't imagine. How must he have felt when his wife deserted him?' She shook her head. 'Nevertheless, he can't have fallen for that other woman in such a short time. He's been crazy about you for years.'

Katie sat up and stared at her aunt. 'What did you say?'

'You heard me. He's been dotty over you since you were a teenager. Indecent, I thought.'

'He's never, in all the years I've known him, said he loved me,' Katie admitted, her eyes fixed on her aunt's face.

'Maybe he's more reserved than I give him credit for. I always thought him a wild, willful young man. Almost brash. Do you love him?'

'Yes.' Katie knew that with great certainty.

'And how often do you tell him?'

Katie was silent, her eyes dropped to the teacup gripped in her hand. She didn't ever remember telling him. Maybe when they'd first married. But then, she had been so in awe of him when she was younger, she couldn't remember if she had ever had the nerve, nor felt he would have welcomed her love. Their life together had been so...so correct.

During the last few years, she didn't know if she loved him. It was nothing like what she felt for him now, the emotion she rediscovered on Key West.

The minutes dragged by and Katie finally looked up at her aunt, meeting her gaze reluctantly. 'I can't remember.'

'So tell him now.'

'I couldn't! I couldn't just go up to him and say "Michael, I love you, don't divorce me". Not after all the times I've insisted that's what I want.'

'False pride,' Margaret snapped.

'Maybe.' Katie carefully placed the teacup and saucer on the coffee table. 'But I made this mess; I have to see it through.' She winced at the pain in her heart, at the thought of the long, lonely years that stretched out ahead of her.

'Do you plan to be happy with it?' her aunt asked.

'I'll get over it,' Katie said forlornly.

The silence in the room stretched out endless minutes. Margaret sipped her tea, looking at her unhappy niece. Finally she took a deep breath.

'We have never been close, Katie. I'm not a warm woman. Not the way your mother was. My brother loved her so much. I was so sorry to lose them together, but I don't think Thomas would ever have been happy again if your mother had died before him. You're all I have left of family now.'

'I know.' Katie felt a wave of love for her aunt. She'd done the best she could for the little orphaned niece she'd been left to care for. She'd never married, never had children of her own. Katie felt her heart sink. Would her life be like that? With not even a niece to share it with?

'Let me tell you something, Katie, something not very many people in the world know. I was not always the old maiden lady you know. Once I was young and pretty—not beautiful the way you are, just passably pretty. But stuck up in my own consequence.'

Margaret carefully placed her cup and saucer on the table, beside Katie's. Folding the napkin primly in her lap, she concentrated on making the folds precise, straight.

'There was a dashing young man who courted me. He was handsome, fun to be with. But poor. Poor with a dream of doing great things. His family was no one in particular. Not good enough for a Harrington of Boston. So I rejected his suit and he left.'

Katie stared at her aunt. She had not known she had had such a chance at happiness.

'He made good. Did fine in his field—electronics research, years ago when it was a brand new field. Several years later, he called me, wanted to get together again, just to meet for old times' sake. I said no. To this day I regret it. I have missed him every day of my life. It was my foolish pride that made me say no in the first place, that refused to let me see him again, if only for an afternoon. I've always wondered how that would have turned out.'

Her eyes met Katie's briefly, then she looked away, sadness in their depths.

'I heard some years later that he finally married and moved to California. I thought my heart would break. I was foolish. If I had anything to do over again, I would never have sent him away. Or, at the very least, I would have met him that spring day when he called me. Don't let foolish pride ruin your life, Katie. If Michael won't call you, you go to him. Take a risk; it may pay off in the greatest happiness you can know.'

'And if it doesn't?'

'Then you know deep within yourself that you tried. You did all you could do, and it was not meant to be. But to not try, to always wonder, it's a hard burden to carry, Katie. I know—I've carried it for decades.'

Katie was silent. It must have been hard for her aunt to tell her that story. She reached over and gave her a hug. Maybe tomorrow, or the next day, when she got her nerve up, she'd approach Michael.

'How long are you planning to stay?' she asked Aunt Margaret.

Margaret surveyed the small apartment, her eyes quizzical. 'If you only have the one bedroom, I don't plan to stay long at all. Where do you propose to put me?'

'You can have the bedroom, I'll sleep on the sofa. It opens up.'

'I could stay at the hotel.'

'No, stay with me. It will be quite different from what you're used to, but it will broaden your horizons.'

Katie smiled at her aunt, trying to imagine her at the pizza place, or playing volleyball on the beach—failing totally. Still, she would introduce her to her friends and see what happened.

Dinner was casual. Margaret brought Katie up to date on all the happenings in Boston, which Katie listened to with only half an ear. She kept thinking of her aunt's story and her own growing desire to speak to Michael. Would it do any good, or was she just setting herself up for more heartache?

'Did you hear a word I said?' Margaret asked.

Katie blinked and grinned sheepishly at her aunt. 'I think so. I was—'

'I know what you were thinking about, or rather who. You used to moon after him when he was courting you.'

'What an old-fashioned term.' Katie laughed.

'But true. Michael is a bit old-fashioned. He asked me for permission to court you.'

Katie was surprised. 'I never knew that.'

'I told him no. I didn't think he had enough for a Harrington.'

'Aunt Margaret! You didn't!'

'I did, and it worked out fine. He said he'd do anything he had to do to get you. He made himself a mint while you were in finishing school. Don't know how he did it, but he came to me shortly before you came home and took me to his house. It was worthy of a Harrington. I gave my permission to court you. He was crazy about you, Katie.'

She put down her fork, suddenly sick. 'Aunt Margaret, I never liked that house.'

'What do you mean? It's a show place.'

'That's right, a show place. But not a home. I thought it was Michael's and he loved it.'

'It is his. He bought it to prove to me he could care for you in the manner you needed.'

'I'll go tonight,' Katie said out loud, surprising herself. Her heart ached for the young man who had done so much just to prove to her aunt that he was worthy of her. And she had thrown it in his face. Could she ever make things right? At least she could let him know she appreciated his efforts.

She showered away the salt water and conditioned her hair. When she dried it, the curls were soft and bright, bleached almost white by the hot southern sun. She used make-up sparingly. In the light she could still see the swollen lids from her tears, but maybe the light at the hotel would be subdued and he wouldn't notice.

Satisfied she looked her best, she rejoined her aunt.

'You're sure you don't mind me leaving you alone your first evening here?' she asked.

'Just run along. I'll look around on my own, go to bed early. You can tell me in the morning how things went. You look pretty, Katie.'

'Thank you, Aunt Margaret. And thank you for coming down.' She gave her aunt a kiss and hug.

Almost light-hearted, Katie walked along Duval Street towards the Monarch Hotel and Michael. She was scared he wouldn't want to talk to her, but was willing to take the risk. If he said no, at least she would have tried. And if he said yes—

She couldn't picture it. Only how awful she would feel if he said no. Yet what else did she expect? He'd asked her more than once to forget the divorce, to try again with him, to take that cruise, or return to Boston, and each time she'd refused. How often had she told him no? And finally he seemed to accept what she said and changed his interests to Elizabeth. Why should he say anything different now?

How she was going to approach it she hadn't a clue. Hoping something would occur to her before she met him, she continued walking. Surely the right words would come when she saw him.

The soft air of Key West caressed her skin as she walked towards the Gulf. The bars spilled out their faint lights and the loud noise from the bands and combos playing for the crowds. Gaiety and happiness radiated from the people crowding the pavements. Most of these people were tourists, on holiday, having a wonderful time. Katie envied their happiness. Would she ever know such happiness again?

The knock on his door went unanswered. She waited another minute and rapped again. Nothing.

She looked up and down the hall. He was probably out with Elizabeth. Her heart dropped. She was a fool. He'd found someone else. He had tried to make that clear to her. She was stupid to think he still wanted her. Hadn't today on the boat proved that?

She turned and started down the hall. He was out and there was no use pretending he'd want to be with her. She'd had a second chance and thrown it away.

Her aunt's words tumbled about in her head. She might never get the courage again. It was tonight, or she would end her years alone, wondering what might have happened had she seen Michael.

She took a deep breath, and turned back. Pausing by his door, she used her passkey and slipped into his room. She would wait for Michael and talk to him tonight. She only hoped he wouldn't bring Elizabeth back with him.

11

Katie left the lights off, wandered out on to the balcony and sat in one of the chairs. The night was quiet, the soft murmur of voices from the patio dining rooms of the hotel rose in a muted background. The rustle of the evening breeze through the palm trees was soothing. She sat and thought and waited, while the normal activities of Key West went on around her.

In the distance, across the water, she saw the lights of a boat, someone sailing on the evening tide, gliding across the water beyond the sound of the land, off to destinations unnamed. She smiled, dreaming of adventure, remembering the boat trips to the coral reef she'd taken. Her smile faded at the remembrance of today's trip.

Michael wasn't indifferent to her. Of that she was sure. But was he mad at her, trying to punish her for her leaving, or did he still want her as a man wanted a woman? His touch inflamed, his eyes burned into her, but he never spoke of love, never of a future. He wanted her to return, but to what? And did he want her any more since he'd met Elizabeth?

She didn't think so, or why would he be out with Elizabeth now?? For a day or two he had been everywhere she'd been. Then his attentions had turned.

He had started seeing Elizabeth. Did he kiss her in the darkness, make love to her? Katie's palms grew damp at the thought and she rubbed them on her dress. She felt sick to her stomach and her heart began pounding unbearably. She'd go mad thinking such thoughts. And she'd have no reason to complain if it were true. She had told him over and over that she wanted to end their marriage. If he had finally believed her, she had only herself to blame.

The evening drew on, and the music from the bars and dance-floors drifted past her. She wore no watch so had no idea how late it was. Had she sat here for minutes only, or endless hours? It felt like days.

When the key sounded in the lock, she panicked. It was too soon. The door opened and Michael switched on the light. Katie looked over her shoulder; he was alone. She stood up, scraping the chair slightly as she did so.

His attention was immediately drawn to the balcony. She stepped to the doorway.

'Hello, Michael.'

'Katie? What are you doing here?'

She stepped inside and laid the master key on the table by the sliding door. 'You said I held the key, so I used it,' she said nervously.

He moved and flicked on the light by the table. She looked away, its brightness dazzling her after the hours on the dark balcony. But he reached out and drew her into the light, his eyes studying her face. She tried to look away, but his fingers caught her chin, tilted her to his gaze.

'Crying, Katie?' he asked so softly, so gently that she almost started again.

'I had a headache,' she prevaricated.

'Liar.' He leaned over and brushed her lips lightly with his. 'Why?' His hands cupped her face, his thumbs tracing her eyes lightly; he kissed her again, lightly, softly.

'Things have been awful lately,' she whispered, hurt and pain evident in her face.

'Isn't that too bad? Did you ever give a thought to the hell you put me through last October?' he said tightly.

She shook her head, her heart aching for the pain she'd caused. 'I didn't think you'd care. You had your business, spent so much time on it that I didn't even think you'd miss me, except at parties if you needed a hostess.'

'I cared. I was stunned when you left. I couldn't believe it had happened. Then I became frantic with worry when I couldn't find you. I had men all over searching for you. What if something happened to you?' His eyes burned down into hers, dark and angry. 'I finally concluded you'd run off with some man, even though you denied it.' His voice was hard, tight with anger.

She shook her head again, as much as his hands would allow. 'There was no other man. There is no other man.'

'Why are you here?' He released her and moved to stand by the sliding door, gazing out into the night.

It wasn't easy; she shouldn't have come. She looked at the door. Should she just give up and leave? She took a breath then turned towards him, her heart pounding. She didn't want to end up like her Aunt Margaret— always regretting the past, wondering how things might have been different. He was so dear to her that she had to try. If she failed, she'd have no one but herself to blame, but at least she would know she had tried to make it work. Since she had caused the breach in the first place, it was up to her to fix it.

'Why are you selling the house?' She said the first thing that occurred to her.

'Why not? You said you didn't like it. That you weren't planning to return. Why keep it? What do you want, Katie? Why are you here?' He turned to look at her through hard, dark eyes.

She stalled, afraid to face the final moment.

'Did you take Elizabeth to dinner?' she asked fiddling with the key on the table.

'What I do with my time is my own business—I believe you made that perfectly clear to me. You still haven't told me why you're here.'

She took a chance. 'I came to stay the night.' She held her breath, her hands damp with nervousness, her heart beating frantically. What would he say? Would he laugh at her, send her on her way, or let her stay?

Michael's face was hard, ruthless. 'Why, so I'll give Jim his recommendation? The ante just went up. Two nights.'

Katie's face flamed at the suggestion, but she held her ground, her own anger rising. How dared he think such a thing about her? Didn't he know her any better? He was judging her without foundation. She had told him she didn't care about Jim except as a friend. Was Michael deliberately baiting her?

She would not be bested. Maybe she'd give him his two nights. Could she gauge his feelings from that? Was he only out to torment her? Wasn't there some feeling for her in him? Her aunt said he'd always been crazy about her. Was Aunt Margaret right? Katie would find out tonight.

Always able to mask her feelings, she put on a smile, and moved seductively towards him, instinct taking over. Let him think what he would—she would buy time to convince him she didn't want to go. She would not let her anger rule; this was too important to her. It was her last chance. She had to succeed.

His eyes were drawn to her dress, to her body swaying towards him. The distance wasn't great, but Katie felt as if it were a mile. Her nerves were raw and she felt suspended over a huge chasm—one false step and life would end.

'No bra?' he asked sardonically.

'Nothing on at all underneath,' she said provocatively, pushing up against him.

Please, don't let him reject me, she prayed silently.

'What are you trying to do to me?' His voice was quiet, but it held anguish and pain. His fists were clenched at his side.

'I'm trying to seduce you, you stupid man! I love you and want you and don't know how else to say it!' She almost yelled the words.

And for the second time that day Katie burst into tears.

'Oh, sweetheart.' Michael gathered her into his arms, drawing her tight against his body, holding her as she rested her head on his chest and cried, his hands stroking her hair, her cheek, her back.

'Don't cry, please, Katie; I don't want to see you this way. Please don't cry.'

She grew quiet, but refused to move. She didn't want to face him. Didn't want to move away from the strength of his chest, the solid feel of him. Didn't want to leave the heaven of his touch, the haven of his arms. She wanted only to remain standing where she was, in his arms, until time ended.

His hand forced her face up to his. 'Say that again,' he ordered, his eyes ablaze with light.

Her lips trembled; he hadn't put her away, he still held her with one arm. Dared she repeat it? Her heart beat heavily with hope.

'What? Stupid man?' she said with rising confidence.

He smiled, wiping a tear from her cheek.

'You may be right. But the next part.'

'I'm trying to seduce you?'

'I'm glad, but that's not the part I mean.'

She licked her lips, afraid to say it again, yet wanting to shout it from the rooftops. 'I love you,' she whispered.

He closed his eyes, and rested his forehead against hers.

'Again.' His voice was so low, she almost didn't hear it.

'I love you, Michael Donovan,' she said loud and clear.

'I love you, Katie Harrington-Donovan. You put me through hell and I still adore you!'

With that his mouth found hers and kissed her so hard that he hurt. His arms bound her to him so tightly that she couldn't breathe. But she didn't care; joy and happiness welled up within her and spilled over.

Michael Donovan loved her.

He reached down to pick her up in his arms and moved to sit on the edge of the bed, Katie on his lap. He kissed her again, his arm around her waist caressing her, while his other hand ran up her leg, beneath her dress.

'Good grief, you really don't have anything on under your dress!' His fingers caressed the soft satin of her hip.

She smiled shyly at him, trailing kisses along his mouth, across his cheek. 'I told you I didn't,' she said in a low voice.

'I can't believe you're here.' His hand slowly rubbed up and down.

'Aunt Margaret sent me. No, that's not quite true. She's here, in Key West. What she said to me tonight showed me I had to talk to you—tonight. I wanted to talk to you before, last week on your balcony. But Elizabeth interrupted.'

'What's Margaret doing here?'

'I wrote to her, and I think I let some of my confusion show; anyway she came down to set me straight,' Katie explained.

'And did she?'

'A little.' Katie traced his lips with her index finger, slipping it in to rub the soft inner lip. He took her finger gently in his teeth and bit her, laving it with his tongue. She smiled sleepily into his eyes. 'She said you were crazy about me. Is that true?'

'She's right.' His eyes were steady, his gaze firm.

'For how long?'

'Since I first saw you. At the Digbys' place, in Cambridge. You must have been about seventeen or so.'

She looked perplexed, trying to remember.

'I was a construction worker. When I saw you, I thought the pot of gold had been given to me. But your Aunt Margaret was too protective of her ewe lamb, and let me know in no uncertain terms I was not good enough for her precious niece.'

'I don't remember.'

'No, I don't suppose you do.' He smiled and shook his head. 'I slaved night and day for three years. Bought that house and furnished it, making it as showy as I could to prove to your aunt I was good enough for you. My credit was strained to the limit— over, really.'

'That's why you worked so hard when we were first married?' Katie looked stricken. 'Michael, you don't still owe on all that, do you?'

He chuckled. 'No, only the mortgage on the house. Everything else was paid off years ago.'

'I never knew. But why sell it? That's your home.'

'No, it isn't. Where you are is my home. That's just a house in Boston.'

Her heart stopped, then pounded furiously. Had she heard him correctly? Where she was, was his home?

'I only bought it for you, sweetheart,' he told her.

'And I didn't like it.'

'You made that clear,' he said dryly, his hand rubbing her thigh, his eyes gazing into hers.

Her finger moved to unbutton his shirt slowly, each button released before moving on to the next one.

'I was so in awe of you,' she tried to explain. 'You were so good-looking, successful, powerful. I couldn't believe it when you married me. I wanted to be the perfect wife for you. I tried to do what you wanted, but as time went on all we did together

was entertain. I got so tired of that. And you were always working, always away from home, and I never saw you alone. And if
I did you treated me... I don't know, formally, distantly.'

She met his eyes, afraid she'd hurt him again, fear clutching
her heart that he would tell her something she didn't want to
hear. Something that would shatter this delightful moment.
Katie felt safe, loved, and she didn't want anything to change
that.

He tapped her chin. 'Don't look like that. I did treat you
carefully when we first married. You were so young, I was afraid
I'd hurt you, or frighten you. I've loved you for years, Katie,
ached with the need for you, but was afraid I'd give you a disgust
of me if I came on too strong, so I held back.'

She spread his shirt, her hands seeking the warm muscles of
his chest, her nails lightly trailing down, across his nipple. He
took another deep breath, snatching her hands, holding them
firmly together against his skin.

'Our backgrounds are totally different,' he began. 'At first I
was uptight in social settings, even when alone with you. Worried
I'd blow it somehow and you'd leave. Or your Aunt Margaret
would come over and prove herself right—that I wasn't the man
for you.'

'I think we were idiots, both of us,' Katie asserted. 'You un-
der-rated me. I'm not so fragile. Your— umm—advances to me
here in Key West are much more enjoyable than our lovemaking
the last year in Boston. Did Key West liberate you?' she teased.

His hand released hers and moved again against her silky leg,
stopping inches from where she wanted him to be. She looked
deep in his eyes with love and trust. She could only think of his
hand, of the bed on which they were sitting and that they loved
each other.

'Seeing you here, I forgot the formal young woman I married. You looked brown and strong and lusty.'

'Lusty?' She smiled in delight.

'Lusty! I'd been sick with fear with you gone, and what with the relief, I guess—whatever, I just didn't hold back any more. But I've loved you all along, and was delighted when I could see you every day. You were so delicate and beautiful. I worshipped at your feet.'

'Silly.' She kissed him, biting gently on his lower lip, tracing it with her tongue, daring to express her love in ways she hadn't before. 'I don't want worship. I want love, your love. Since you came to Key West, I've not thought of another thing. All you do is touch me, kiss me, and I'm consumed by you. It's glorious.'

She fell silent a moment. When his hand began to move again, she stopped it. A warm glow, tinged with sadness, spread through Katie. Sad for all the time wasted, she looked up at him. 'A lot of time wasted, don't you think?' she said. 'I should never have left you.'

'Not wasted exactly. But a learning experience. That day in Miami, what you were saying finally penetrated. I'd been building Donovan Construction to support you in fine style, the way your aunt wanted. But you didn't care for that; you wanted a family, a mate to share your time with. I rode roughshod over you, thinking I knew best, when all you wanted was to be considered.'

She nodded.

'It's easy, once you stop and listen. You should have made me listen years ago. I'd done it all for you—worked hard, moved ahead, and it wasn't what you wanted. Incredible as it seemed to me, you wanted time, not money. Only, when I put the company in the hands of others, it seemed you still didn't want me.'

'I didn't believe you,' she said. 'For so many years you've put the business first, I just couldn't believe it. Only when you came back, and had nothing further to do with it, did I begin to understand. I don't want you to give up your company, Michael. Not for me. Just don't spend so much time there.' She traced his jaw, daring to peek into his eyes. The warmth and love she saw there caused her heart to beat faster.

'Katie, what we have now is much more powerful than what we had the last few years. I want to spend time with you, want you with me.'

'I never grew completely up in Boston. I was so sheltered. I believe I have grown up here, on my own,' she told him.

'And I'm glad you did.' His hand moved again. 'When we go back, things will be different. I won't spend so much time away from you, so much time on business. I've learned there's more to life than just business. When I thought you'd gone, the company held no meaning for me. I started out to make money for you. With you gone, it holds no appeal.'

'What about Frances?'

'I told you, she's retired. If you need help, you can get it. But for a while I'd like it to be you and me.'

Katie warmed at that thought. Smiling dreamily, she envisioned the two of them together. Doing things they both liked, sharing their lives. Only one thing still marred the perfect resolution.

'And Elizabeth?' She had to know.

He smiled. 'Jealous, were we?'

She nodded, her smile rueful.

'Then my plan worked. I was at my wits' end. I tried talking you into a cruise—no go. I tried threats—no go. Even bargaining with you, for Jim's future. Still nothing. Elizabeth was my last ploy. If it hadn't worked, I might have had to believe you—that we were through—and I fought against that.'

This was the man she knew. He was determined, focused,

going after what he wanted with no thoughts to others. For once, Katie was glad he was that way, and that she was what he wanted; but she gave a brief thought to Elizabeth, hoping she would not be deeply hurt by Michael's actions.

'But you bought her a bracelet.' She closed her eyes when the words slipped out. How could she tell him that?

His chuckle opened her eyes. He stood her on her feet and motioned to the dressing table.

'Top right-hand drawer. Go on, look.'

She opened the drawer and drew out the black velvet pouch. Spilling the contents out to her hand, she smiled at the delicate conches strung together to make the bracelet. She looked over at him.

'I thought they were pretty; I wanted them for you,' he said simply.

She walked over to the table by the window and snapped off the light.

'What about the house?' she asked.

'The old one's for sale. We'll decide where we want to live and buy a house together.' His eyes followed her as she walked to the wall-switch; one strap of the dress had fallen from her shoulder and the tanned skin glowed in the remaining light.

'And furnish it together, too?' She snapped off that light.

'As long as you make it as welcoming as your apartment,' he said.

The soft light reflected through the sliding door enabled Katie to see her way to where Michael sat.

'One more thing,' she said as she drew to a halt before him.

He reached up and slid the other strap of her dress down her shoulders, slowly peeling the dress from her.

'Babies,' he said.

'Babies?' She was surprised; that had not been what she was going to say.

'I want lots of babies with you, sweetheart. Ever since you said that at the restaurant, I've thought of little else. I want to make babies with you and only you, Katie. We'll fill our house with them, starting tonight, maybe.'

He stood beside her, shrugging out of his shirt, and reaching for her warm, welcoming body. She felt as if she had come home. This was Michael, the man she had left to find again. Happiness and joy would be hers now and forever. She hadn't lost him, after all, but had gained even more with him now than they had ever known in Boston. Their future looked bright. They would love each other, share their lives together and build a family conceived in love.

'The divorce?' she said just before his mouth covered hers.

He stopped, his lips only inches above hers.

'Oh, that—well... I told the attorneys to forget it when I came back to Key West. What I have, I hold...'

If you liked **Island Rendezvous**,
you'll love book 2 in the Tropical Escape series,
Come Into The Sun.

You can find all Barbara McMahon's books
on her website at barbaramcmahon.com.

www.ingramcontent.com/pod-product-compliance
Lightning Source LLC
Chambersburg PA
CBHW070549180626
46817CB00005B/1760